SURPRISE
AT
SPANISH BAY

OTHER BOOKS BY MICHAEL DOVE

CRIM 279
THE RUNNING LIFE (WITH DONALD BURAGLIO)
PARADOX AT PEBBLE BEACH
CONFUSION AT CYPRESS POINT
SUSPICION AT SPYGLASS HILL

SURPRISE
AT
SPANISH BAY

MICHAEL DOVE

SURPRISE AT SPANISH BAY

iUniverse books may be ordered through booksellers or by contacting:

iUniverse
1663 Liberty Drive
Bloomington, IN 47403
www.iuniverse.com
844-349-9409

ISBN: 978-1-6632-6259-2 (sc)
ISBN: 978-1-6632-6260-8 (e)

Library of Congress Control Number: 2024908947

Print information available on the last page.

iUniverse rev. date: 05/06/2024

"This is one of my favorite spots on earth here at Pebble Beach. Spyglass Hill and Pebble Beach are two of my favorite golf courses, and Spanish Bay probably has the best views of any golf course I've ever seen."

Senior PGA Tour Professional - Scott McCarron

"It was as though we had been chosen by the Pope to make a sculpture in the Vatican of golf."

The Links at Spanish Bay course co-designer - Sandy Tatum

"Our goal is to produce a final product that will be in the top echelon of 'must play' courses."

Golf Course Architect chosen to renovate the Links at Spanish Bay
- Gil Hanse

FOREWORD

How We Built The Links at Spanish Bay

Posted in *Golf, Centennial* on October 9, 2019
Robert Trent Jones, Jr.

A look back at the construction of one of California's top-rated golf courses by Robert Trent Jones, Jr.

In the early 1980s, I competed to be the architect for neighboring Poppy Hills Golf Course in the upper forest of Pebble Beach and won. While working on the Poppy Hills project, I also kept an eye on the former sand mine site along the north border of Pebble Beach near Asilomar. I just had to make a run at this once-in-a-decade site, so I consulted with Sandy Tatum, my San Francisco Club friend and president of the USGA, who was a close friend of Tom Watson.

We all met and agreed to collaborate. The game was on.

Approving Spanish Bay

Tom, who had never designed a course, along with Sandy and our team, walked the site, pondering our plans while playing golf together several times – specifically at Cypress Point Club and the early holes of Spyglass Hill Golf Course.

We enjoyed many dinners at The Lodge, sharing our visions for the project, and eventually walked the site to determine the layout that ownership would need to approve in coordination with building the residences at The Inn at Spanish Bay.

With owner endorsement, our plans were submitted to Monterey County officials and the California Coastal Commission for approval. The golf course design was based on a links, dunescape concept, and the plan gained support from non-golfers because of the dune restoration at the existing mined-out area.

After a heavily attended, all-day Coastal Commission hearing, the project was approved by a close vote. And then the fun began – actually getting to build a great new course.

Deciding the Design

Naturally, there were many passionate discussions onsite on fine golfing points.

Tom wanted smaller, well-placed bunkers and interesting spill-off chipping areas, and strong green contours reminiscent of the links courses along the seas of the British Isles.

Sandy favored more penal targets off the tee, particularly adding bunkers along the right side of No. 6, which we affectionately named "Sandy."

I was interested in providing strategic options throughout the course, with wide but contoured fairways providing different angles for the approach shots to the green. Thus we introduced many split fairways, bisected by central bunkers such as holes 5, 10, 11 and 14.

The course is mostly open to the Pacific Ocean and the elements, the prevailing winds, or what we liked to call "invisible hazards." We carefully thought through how the weather would affect every golf shot. We had a great time. Sandy said, "It was as though we had been chosen by the Pope to make a sculpture in the Vatican of golf."

During a lengthy meeting at The Lodge in July before it opened, near the time of the British Open, ownership decided to call the course "The Links at Spanish Bay," based on what the area had been called for centuries.

Tom observed that he couldn't wait to play it, and could "almost hear the bagpipes." Thus, the bagpiping rituals at sunset and the logo were born.

Looking back, we miss Sandy Tatum and his extreme dedication to the game. When the bagpipes play in the evening, we know he is here with us in spirit at The Links at Spanish Bay.

THE LINKS AT SPANISH BAY COURSE

HOLE 1: To the Sea 500 yards Par 5

HOLE 2: Straight and Narrow 307 yards Par 4

HOLE 3: Pitch and Run 340 yards Par 4

HOLE 4: Shepherd's Haven 190 yards Par 3

HOLE 5: Blind Choice 451 yards Par 4

HOLE 6: Sandy 400 yards Par 4

HOLE 7: Left Begone 418 yards Par 4

HOLE 8: Marsh Corner 158 yards Par 3

HOLE 9: White Dune 394 yards Par 4

HOLE 10: Half & Half 520 yards Par 5

HOLE 11: Top Hat 365 yards Par 4

HOLE 12: Cathedral 432 yards Par 4

HOLE 13: Wee Precipice 126 yards Par 3

HOLE 14: Wind & Willow 576 yards Par 5

HOLE 15: Missing Link 390 yards Par 4

HOLE 16: Dune Hollow 200 yards Par 3

HOLE 17: Whale Watch 413 yards Par 4

HOLE 18: Long Home 574 yards Par 5

AUTHOR'S NOTE

The original concept when I started writing these Chipper Blair and Jenny Nelson golf, suspense, romance novels was to have a trilogy: three only. I had the plots of all three novels firmly fixed in my brain, and I had a basic idea of where the stories were going. They would end happily with the marriage of Jenny and Chipper on the seventh green at Pebble Beach Golf Course. That happened in the previous Suspicion at Spyglass Hill novel. But... ...

I thank my many friends and readers who clamored for more Chipper, Jenny, and golf stories. They persuaded me to continue with the golf and suspense and convinced me to do a fourth novel and maybe more. The Pebble Beach Company owns The Links at Spanish Bay as well. It is only natural to do this fourth and, unexpected-by-me, novel, centered on the Links at Spanish Bay. I do not have a planned story about it in my head, so what comes in the following pages is a surprise to me. I am hoping inspiration springs, and you find it enjoyable.

I thank the Pebble Beach Company for recently hiring golf architects Gil Hanse and Jim Wagner to do a "renovation" of the golf links as it has given me a new plot line. Also, the golf world has been shaken by the new Saudi-sponsored LIV league, with many players "defecting" to the new league for massive payouts. The rift seems ripe for a story. Let's see where this goes.

THE HONEYMOON IS OVER

When Mr. and Mrs. Walter "Chipper" Blair returned home from their honeymoon in Scotland, their black Scottish terrier Angus was waiting on the front steps of their Pebble Beach Golf Course estate home. They were expected and were on time. Alongside Angus was Irene McVay.

Mrs. Blair, Jenny Nelson, also known as Shoshona Jennifer Nelsberg was overjoyed and content to be married to Chipper. They were both very much in love. Jenny had decided to keep her maiden name because she was now the much-requested queen of golf teaching professionals at Pebble Beach and Spyglass Hill golf courses. She was listed as the fourteenth best in the United States in the prestigious yearly rankings list by Golf Digest Magazine.

It was hard to say who was more excited to see them, Angus or Irene. Angus was doing his usual jumping up and down and demanded to alternately be picked up or to roll over and have his belly rubbed. Irene was impatient as well but never jumped up and down and never asked to have her belly rubbed, although the belly rub wasn't beyond something she would ask for. "Tell me about the honeymoon. I want to know all about it, Jenny," Irene said over and over. "I want to hear every detail."

Chipper slumped his shoulders and reluctantly started bringing the two suitcases they had taken and carrying them up the stairs to their bedroom. Chipper Blair was slim, and just under six feet tall with slightly longish messy hair and a ragged mustache. He had to trim it the next morning before he went to work. Jenny Nelson was a few inches shorter than Chipper, also slim, with dark black hair, a figure Chipper loved, and classically beautiful with a dark complexion and flickering green eyes. Jenny went into the kitchen and tried to answer Irene McVay's probing questions.

Irene was a fifty-nine-year-old widow, who lived in her own large estate off the eleventh fairway at Pebble Beach Golf Course. Her current boyfriend, Big Bill O'Shea, slept over several nights a week. She was just getting to know the new tenant in her guest house, who was a twenty-four-year-old student at the Monterey Institute of International Studies. Chipper had lived in her guest house for some time and provided services, both household and sexual, to Irene, before he met Jenny. Irene was straightforward with no boundaries or inhibitions. When Chipper and Jenny were gone, Angus often trotted over to Irene's house and slept with her and Bill, and enjoyed the food she gave him. When she didn't see Angus for a few days, she headed over to Chipper's (and now Jenny's) estate off the fourteenth fairway, to see how Angus was getting along. He was a very independent and resourceful little dog: very intelligent.

Irene asked again, "So Jenny, tell me about everything. Tell me about your honeymoon. Don't leave out any details."

Jenny, although tired from the trip, started, "We had a wonderful time. This time we drove ourselves. We didn't rent a limo or a tour guide like last time. Chipper drove some of the time, and I did when he was tired...."

Irene injected, "Did you wear him out in bed? Is that why he was tired? Tell me, Jenny-girl."

"I'm not going to tell you about what we did in bed, Irene. That's between Chipper and me. It was our honeymoon, you know."

"Then I don't want to hear any more. Make it interesting for me, Jenny."

"Let me finish my story, then. We started in Anstruther, where we have new friends from our last trip. The golf pro Mack and other townspeople. We stayed in the same hotel as before and went to the same taverns. The Dreel is what our own bar downstairs is modeled after, you know? It felt like home. There was a party for us at the golf course..."

"Come on, Jenny. Give me the dish. Did you have sex all the time?"

"Irene, you are incorrigible. You know we lived together a long time before we got married. Yes. Chipper was very attentive. We made love usually every morning when we woke up and when we went to bed at night. It was very nice. We cuddled and talked a lot, too. Chipper is a surprising guy. He acts like he cares about nothing but golf, but he knows a lot about everything. He is very smart. We had some great bedtime conversations: how many kids we want, our philosophies of life, what we like and what we don't like, religion, God, friendship, meaning of life, really a lot of stuff that I don't think most couples ever talk about."

"When I'm in bed, I just like to think about sex. Not much talk."

"I know, Irene. We also went to a lot of good restaurants, although Scotland isn't known for good food, but we ate well, and drank well, and had a good time. We even did some sightseeing: distilleries, lochs, castles, historical sights, hiking, saw a lot of Scottie dogs. It was really wonderful."

"How many different positions did you use for sex?"

"That, Irene, is none of your business."

"Big Bill and I are up to sixteen different ones. I keep track in my diary. Chipper was reluctant with me, so it was usually me on top prodding him, so we didn't have too many. I hope he was more inventive with you."

"Way too much information, Irene. Really, can't you keep this stuff to yourself? You have no filter at all. I'm not going to tell you anything more about sex." Jenny made a zipping-the-lips motion with her hand.

3

"So, tell me about the food then, Jenny. I want to hear all about the restaurants."

"Let's do this another time, Irene. Now that we're back, we hope to settle into a routine and just have a quiet time for the next several months: me, teaching, and Chipper, back at his beloved driving range. No drama. Just relaxation and doing what we love to do. I should help Chipper unpack, and I am really tired, too."

Irene followed Jenny up the stairs to the bedroom and asked if she could help with anything. By the time they got upstairs, Angus had comfortably burrowed in under the covers. Chipper had taken Jenny's clothes out of the suitcase and spread them out, so Jenny could decide what got hung up, and what got put in drawers, and what went into the dirty laundry. Chipper was exhausted, but Irene talked him into sitting outside on the bedroom deck and answering some more questions.

It was a beautiful evening, and the sun had gone down, but they could see the moon and the reflection off Carmel Bay in the distance and the very green fourteenth fairway just beyond their back yard. Chipper was looking forward to hitting their Ben Morris shot in the morning and playing his way into work on Pebble Beach's moist morning fairways. He was in his element again and was looking forward to several months of sameness, just working his driving range, and playing some golf.

Irene started, "So, Chipper. Tell me about the honeymoon. How was the sex? Jenny told me all about it."

Chipper said wearily, "I doubt that she did, Irene. We had a wonderful honeymoon. We played Anstruther several times. We played the Old Course at St. Andrews three times. The weather cooperated most of the time, even though this is the coldest time of the year. We got to play some of the courses I have always wanted to play: Cruden Bay, Turnberry, Prestwick, Dornoch in the way-up north, Inverness, Muirfield, North Berwick, Gullane number two, Kingsbarns, Carnoustie. I absolutely love the old-style courses, North Berwick is the most fun to play. Cruden Bay is incredible. Prestwick is fun. We had a great time."

"I don't care about your golf, Chipper. Tell me about you and Jenny and where you ate and what you saw."

"I loved Prestwick. I was under par. It's a really great old golf course. The holes there and at North Berwick are really interesting. I shot under par at Prestwick…"

"Enough with the golf, Chipper. Just enough. I'm done with you. Jenny was more fun to talk to. She's always better to talk to than you."

"OK. Then can I go inside? I'm tired, and I have to go to work in the morning. I want to go to work in the morning."

Chipper and Irene went in the bedroom, and Jenny was just finishing cleaning up. Angus couldn't be seen, but there was an obvious lump under the covers.

Irene commented as she was leaving, "Oh, yes. I forgot to tell you. You have some new neighbors next door. I noticed several of them in the yard a few days back. They seemed to be carrying rugs and kneeling down on them. Several people."

ANGUS ON ALERT

Mr. and Mrs. Chipper Blair slept poorly. They started to make love, but Angus would have none of it. He was all over them, licking, cuddling, and just excited that they were home and sleeping with him. They finally gave up and rolled over and tried to sleep. Angus alternately nudged each of them looking for belly and head rubs.

In the morning, Chipper and Jenny were up early and ready to go, but Angus was still under the covers, reluctant to get out of the comfortable bed. Chipper said, "Angus is getting lazy. Should we just leave him here?" Then he answered his own question by dragging Angus out of the bed. Angus was unusually slow in walking down the steps to the back door and kept looking up at Jenny and Chipper with a begging look on his face. He appeared afraid to go outside when they exited the back door and headed down to the back lawn. It was a clear morning with no fog or wind. Jenny had to coax Angus down the steps.

Angus was looking around toward the new neighbors' home down the fairway closer to the fourteenth green. The estate homes were a good one hundred yards apart, but Angus looked apprehensive. When they reached the patch of fescue grass with their brassie and long spoon, Angus was keeping very close to Jenny's legs and keeping her between him and the direction of the neighbors. He was whimpering.

Jenny exclaimed, "What's up, Angus? Are you OK? You are worrying me. Did something happen when we were gone? Where is your energy?"

Chipper had to hold Angus to the side while Jenny put down her Slazenger golf ball and took some practice swings. Poor Angus was shaking. When Jenny hit her shot, Chipper was expecting Angus to take off with his usual energy, but he just lay in the grass near Chipper's foot. Both Jenny and Chipper were worried and prompted Angus to run toward the green and pick up the Slazenger. Jenny didn't even make a comment about where the ball would be on the green, because she was worried about Angus's lack of response. Finally they both pushed him toward the green, and he took off very fast. Angus was looking toward the neighbors' back yard the entire start of his run.

Before Angus had travelled fifty yards, Chipper and Jenny saw the reason for the dog's apprehension. They saw three Doberman Pinschers and one husky Pit bull in the neighbors' yard snarling, barking, and furiously running toward the poor black dog. Chipper and Jenny started running, still holding their golf clubs, as they expected to use them as weapons against the dogs. Angus was now headed away from the direct route to the green and took a ninety-degree turn toward the fourteenth fairway. Before Chipper and Jenny had run more than ten yards they saw the four dogs reach the side of their estate lawn, and each looked like they had run into a wall. Each stopped abruptly, two of them yelped in obvious pain and discomfort, the other two whimpered and rolled on the ground. The dogs stepped back, obviously stopped by an invisible electric fence. Chipper noticed that the dogs had collars on their necks that obviously zapped them when they approached the end of the property.

When Angus heard the dogs yelping, he stopped and turned, looked very happy, and then headed toward the green. On his way back, with the Slazenger in his mouth, Chipper and Jenny were amused that Angus didn't come directly back but walked slowly near the border of the neighbors' estate in what looked like a purposeful attempt to taunt the much bigger and angrier dogs. One of them made a run at Angus and again was zapped with what must have been a powerful jolt of electricity, as he hit the ground again and slinked away slowly. All four dogs were barking and snarling. Angus continued his apparent taunting.

Chipper was reluctant to hit his shot, as he didn't want to go through the trauma again, but Angus was anxious to run this time. He thought to himself, and was sure Jenny was thinking the same thoughts: *What if for some reason the electric fence isn't working or the new neighbors forget to activate it? Why do they need the four obviously aggressive dogs?*

Chipper hit a great shot that was no more than three feet from the hole. Jenny looked through the telescope and verified it. She barely had time to get up the stairs to check the telescope before a very fast Angus scooped up the ball and turned to bring it back. He again approached the fence and walked slowly by as two of the dogs again got shocked by electricity. Angus was not making friends.

Chipper said, "Jenny, we have to visit the neighbors and figure out who they are and talk about those dogs. I'll take a break during the day and see if I can go talk to Richard and find out who bought the house and what they are about. This isn't good. Not good at all."

As they were driving out to the fairway to play their way into work, they noticed three men in business suits walking from the house next door to the back yard to see what the dogs were yelping about. Luckily, Angus wasn't in sight. He had taken off toward Irene McVay's a minute before.

PEBBLE BEACH COMPANY MEETING

Donald Stevens, the CEO of the Pebble Beach Company had been holding morning meetings daily for the past week regarding the PGA Tour ATT Pro-Am that would be held at Pebble Beach Golf Course and Spyglass Hill Golf Course in just over two weeks. Monday, January 29th through Wednesday, January 31st would be practice rounds, then the tournament proper would run Thursday, February 1st through Sunday, February 4th. He was planning on morning daily meetings through the end of the tournament.

It was a special year for the ATT Pro-Am. This year it was a "Signature Event" with a twenty million dollar purse for the pro golfers. The field was limited to only eighty of the best professionals: the top fifty players in the world, based on last year's FedEx points list as well as those who earned FedEx points in the Fall and Winter tour to move into the top seventy on the list, as well as those who were in the top ten in the points list in the current 2024 year. The whole golf world would be focused on Pebble Beach and the Del Monte Forest.

It was a big change from previous years. Instead of amateurs, many of them celebrities, playing three complete days, then the best playing on Sunday in the Pro-Am, now the amateur partners would only play Thursday and Friday. The field of the best eighty pros in the world would get to play all four days without the usual cut after Friday's round. Instead of three courses being used, only Pebble and Spyglass would be used on Thursday and Friday, and only Pebble on Saturday and Sunday.

There were only four other "Signature Events" on the entire tour in 2024: The Tournament of Champions at Kapalua, the RBC Heritage, the Wells Fargo, and the Travelers. This was a big deal for the PGA Tour and Pebble Beach. CEO Stevens wanted to make sure it was perfect. The actual Clambake would still be held on Tuesday night: historically a huge party and banquet for all participants with entertainment provided by celebrities who were playing in the tournament. It would be held, as usual, in the Lodge. The Clambake was started almost ninety years before when Bing Crosby started the tournament for his friends in 1937.

Stevens started the meeting on time, "Thank you, everyone, for being on time. We have two weeks until tournament week begins with practice rounds on the twenty-ninth. I'm happy to say we have all the tents and stands and infrastructure in place now. The contractor finished yesterday, right on time. We'll have TV people wandering around for the next few weeks getting their stuff together. This is a big deal. Some pros and amateurs will be coming in for some extra practice rounds before tournament week. Many like to play the other courses, too, besides Pebble and Spyglass. I cannot emphasize enough how much we have to make all this work without any issues at all. Does anyone have anything regarding the tournament that they want to discuss?"

There were no comments at all, and Stevens continued, "I can't believe there are no issues, or are you all just tired today? The other stuff going on is that Gil Hanse and crew are over at Spanish Bay looking over the course and doing measurements for the renovation. We want to give them every courtesy. The course is still open for play. Anyone have any comments on that?"

Again there was complete silence.

"OK. My last issue may seem petty to some of you, but I understand that Chipper Blair and his new wife Jenny Nelson are back from their honeymoon. I hear she has refused our offer to switch to the golf academy and just wants to teach at Spyglass Hill. Also, she wants to limit her lessons to four or five a day and not on weekends. I'm not happy with any of that, but we'll let her do that for a while and see how it goes. I can't believe so many people will pay fifteen hundred dollars an hour for lessons from her. Wow. And the Corporation keeps half of that. Crazy. Crazy indeed. Now we come to Blair. I want him out of the tournament area, starting now, until the tournament is over. Trouble seems to follow him around. We only keep him on because he's a friend of yours, Roger…"

Head pro at Pebble Beach, Roger Hennessey commented, "He is great at the driving range. He keeps it pristine. No one loves golf more than Chipper. He's just been unfortunate the last year or so with strange events following him…"

Stevens didn't like the interruption, "Let me finish, Roger. I think being involved in several assault and murder cases aren't just unfortunate and strange events. I think his temper and personality get him in trouble. Why does he want to work, anyway? He's got millions."

"He loves golf and being around the golf course, Donald."

"Well, I want him moved to the Links at Spanish Bay for the next three weeks. Keep him out of the Pebble and Spyglass areas. He is just a disaster waiting to happen. I don't think he can get into any trouble over there."

Hennessey said, "There is no driving range over there. He would have to work in the pro shop again, and that never turns out well."

Stevens laughed, "Another reason we should not keep him on. Just tell him he's needed over there for the renovation and to keep Hanse happy, if Hanse has any questions. I'll tell Gil Hanse about that too. Make Blair think he's being moved over there for an important reason. I don't care what you tell him. Just get him out of here. Meeting's over. See you all tomorrow morning. Tell him today, Roger."

Stevens left the room quickly and seemed very unhappy. Richard Stein walked over to Roger and said, "Chipper's not going to take this well, for sure. Look what happened when you moved him to Spyglass."

"I know that, Richard. Don't you think I know that? Maybe he's mellowed since he's now married and just back from his honeymoon?"

Stein smiled and said, "What are the chances, Roger? Just what are the chances of that?"

Donald Stevens never spoke to Gil Hanse. He never had any intention of telling Gil Hanse about Chipper.

PEBBLE BEACH DRIVING RANGE

Chipper had dropped off Jenny at Spyglass and was now in his element at the driving range at Pebble Beach. It was like breathing a big sigh of relief for him to be back where he was the most comfortable. The range shack was his peaceful place. It was like meditation. Nothing to think about at all. Just relax and watch the hacks hit golf balls. Chipper never reflected on why he liked it so much. He just let it happen. Maybe because it made him feel superior to those on the range who couldn't come close to being the golfer he was. Maybe because he was comfortable with his responsibilities there. He enjoyed the beauty of the grass and the trees. He enjoyed the solitude. He was content. At least for thirty minutes.

Roger Hennessey went right to the range after his meeting with CEO Stevens. Might as well get this over with. It would be uncomfortable. Chipper was not surprised to see Roger, as he was best man at Chipper's wedding, and he anticipated Roger would come by to say hello and find out about his trip to Scotland. Hennessey started, "Welcome back, Chipper. How is Jenny? I was just in a meeting with Stevens, and I haven't seen Jenny yet this morning, either. How was your honeymoon?"

"It was great. We played Anstruther several times. We played the Old Course at St. Andrews three times. The weather cooperated most of the time, even though this is the coldest time of the year. We got to play some of the courses I have always wanted to play: Cruden Bay, Turnberry,

Prestwick, Dornoch in the way-up north, Inverness, Muirfield, North Berwick, Gullane number two, Kingsbarns, Carnoustie. I absolutely love the old-style courses, North Berwick is the most fun to play. Cruden Bay is incredible. Prestwick is fun. We had a great time."

"How did you get on Muirfield? It's a tough one to get on."

"Being associated with Pebble Beach is a great in. Every place we went, we were welcomed. Didn't have to pay at a lot of them. We tried to make starting times the day before, but we pretty much just looked at the golf map and went from place to place. January is a strange time to take a golf trip to Scotland, and the courses didn't have many tourists. Just locals who play very fast. It was great. We could play thirty-six on some days."

"Did Jenny enjoy so much golf? When people talk about their honeymoons, they usually don't talk about golf. Did you do other stuff?"

"Jenny enjoyed the golf, and we did some sightseeing, too. Nice restaurants she picked. It's nice to have money, Roger."

"I'll go talk to Jenny after I leave here." Roger hesitated long enough for Chipper to know the other shoe was going to drop.

"Go ahead, Roger, spit it out. I can tell you are trying to tell me something I won't like. It's happened before. You wouldn't be much of a poker player. No poker face. Just tell me."

"You know that Gil Hanse and company are doing a renovation of Spanish Bay. Well, Stevens wants you to be the Pebble Beach liaison to Hanse and his crew. Provide advice. Be there in the planning stages, if they have questions to ask. Give your opinions. Help them out."

"I've always hated the Links at Spanish Bay. Never enjoyed playing there. I'm happy to provide advice. Will Hanse listen to me? I know a lot about golf, but he's a professional architect, and I'm just a golfer with a lot of experience. Lots of opinions about what can be done, too. I guess he'll just call me or come over here if he needs anything? I would be happy to do that. I hope he listens to me."

"Well, about that, Chipper. Stevens wants you to be over there at Spanish Bay, so Hanse can find you any time, and it will be easier for him and his planning crew."

"So I'm supposed to just sit over there and wait for him with questions? I wouldn't mind following him around and seeing how he plans and maps out the new course. Pick his brain. He's one of the best."

"Stevens wants you over there starting today to work in the clubhouse."

"Shit, Roger. They don't even have a driving range over there. I don't want to work in the clubhouse. That never goes well. Look at my Yelp reviews while at Spyglass."

"It's only for three weeks, Chipper. Just three weeks."

Chipper thought awhile then looked at Roger and said, "I'm no dummy, Roger. Stevens thinks I'm cursed and wants me out of the way during the ATT. None of the stuff that happened in the last year was my fault. The Hastings and Golberry are both gone and forgotten. I can't get into any trouble any more. I was looking forward to seeing all the pros and celebrities out here the next several weeks. Really looking forward to it. Spanish Bay is oblivion. Purgatory."

"You can always just come over here and hang around after your work over there. Stevens doesn't control your personal time."

"This is awful, Roger. Who is going to take care of my range? It has to be pristine for the tournament. Certainly don't use kids to do anything. They leave it a mess. No one picks up the balls in the trees or rough. They don't move the tees every day. They don't replace and fix the divots. You have to love the range, and they don't like I do."

"I'll have Big Bill tend range for the next three weeks, Chipper. All I can say is that I know it's a raw deal, but maybe you'll enjoy your learning experience with Hanse. Good luck over there, be careful. I'm going to go talk to Jenny. I'll call Bill and tell him to get over here as fast as he can."

"Please tell her I've been cast into purgatory like in Dante's Inferno for three weeks. UGH. I have to go talk to Richard about a few things, then I'll head over to Hell. I'll be a good boy, Roger. I promise."

"Maybe being married has mellowed you, Chipper?" Roger said, but inside, he doubted it.

Chipper called Jenny then called Richard Stein to see if Stein was in his office. He was, and Chipper hopped in his cart and headed over the short distance to the corporate offices in the Lodge.

RICHARD STEIN

Chipper parked his cart right in the street in front of the Lodge, across the street from the entrance, between a Ferrari and a Lamborghini. There were always two expensive cars parked in those spots. It was intended to let people know this was an expensive place and to make sure visitors were ready to spend money. Chipper didn't know if the cars were owned by the Corporation or were guests' cars that were parked there instead of under the Lodge in the parking lot. He had a hunch they were guests' cars, as they always seemed to be different every time he went there.

Chipper was always impressed when he walked in the front doors of the Lodge. He lingered in the large lounge area on the other side of the entrance to admire the view of the eighteenth green at Pebble and Carmel Bay behind it. He took a quick glance around the large room to see what kind of guests were sipping coffee or having a mid-morning alcoholic pick-me-up. He didn't see anyone wearing Levi's or Gap clothing. Just what rich people wear, or those pretending to be rich. Chipper had on his usual required khaki-color pants and Pebble Beach logo blue shirt. He also wore a matching blue Pebble Beach logo golf cap.

He turned around and walked down the hall and up to the second floor corporate offices. Stein's admin assistant was expecting Chipper and walked him right into Richard's office. Stein was on the phone, as usual, and waved Chipper to take a seat. He mouthed silently with what looked like "This might take a while." Chipper didn't sit down but walked around and admired the same view out the window as he was familiar with downstairs.

Stein was probably talking to another company representative that wanted to provide NIL money to CSUMB golfer Cindy Springer. Stein was her only legal representative and was now getting an outlandish forty percent of the contract money he arranged for her. She already had a dozen contracts based on her internet presence and exposure on golf channel. Stein was saying, "Cindy doesn't need you. She already has contracts with Under Armour and lululemon. She doesn't need another clothing sponsor. She is very comfortable in their outfits and presenting them on Instagram posts. They love her. You would have to come up with a lot more than you are offering in order for her to make a switch to Nike."

When Chipper heard the word Nike, he came over closer to Richard. Richard just winked at him and then said into the phone, "If you want to offer twice what you just offered me, then I'll take it to Cindy, and we'll discuss it. Just call me back tomorrow when you decide." He hung up the phone and said to Chipper, "Can you believe Nike is offering this little girl two million dollars a year just for wearing their clothes? It's absolutely incredible. She plays fourth or fifth girl on a division two golf team, and they want to pay her that much money just for showing their clothes on her internet posts. They don't even want her for commercials or anything like that. I turned down the two million, and I can bet you they will call tomorrow agreeing to my four million. Yesterday, Kim Kardashian's company, Skims, contacted me, and they want her for commercials for their underwear brand. It's crazy. Absolutely crazy. I don't even have to do much. They call me, and I negotiate her more than they offer, always. I sometimes spend more time each day on her rather than my real job. Just because she's a cute little blonde that says whompalicous a lot. Have you seen how many whompalicious and whackalicious energy bars have been selling?"

Chipper commented, "I had one and didn't like it. I have no idea."

Stein gleefully said, "I renegotiated her contract, so she now gets five percent of gross sales. It's amazing how much the little girl makes now. And I need the forty percent. Did I tell you I was the high bidder, one of the only bidders, really, on Emily Hastings' house? She had to do a fire sale, a quick sale, because of Golberry's ruining Hastings Lumber, so I got a good deal. Still, I had to pay sixteen million dollars for the house. She's leaving most of the furniture, too, but I think it's worth at least twenty-five million."

Chipper really wasn't interested but said, "Have you moved in yet? With Debbie?"

"Debbie is anxious to move in. Can you believe it? She once lived in the guest house there, and now she's going to be the co-owner of the house. I put her on the deed. Not sure that was a good idea, but we're getting along great. We haven't moved in, because right when the house sold, I got an offer from a guy who said he wanted to rent the house for the month because he had a group that was coming to the ATT golf. You won't believe what he paid me."

Stein unlocked his bottom right desk drawer and showed Chipper a desk full of money. He took out a bundle of hundred dollar bills wrapped with a rubber band and pointed to several more in the drawer. "He gave me a million dollars cash for the house rental for just a month. Can you believe that?"

The phone rang before Chipper could respond, and Stein picked it up immediately. "Richard Stein, Pebble Beach Company. Can I help you?"

Chipper wasn't in a hurry to get over to Spanish Bay and just wandered around Stein's office. He saw a great number of plaques on the wall given to Richard for saving the Del Monte Forest from tree cutting. Stein was a local hero. Chipper also took some pictures of some aerial view photos of the Del Monte Forest, showing all the golf courses and roads from above.

Stein was now saying, "She is already sponsored by Callaway, and she played well enough with the clubs to make the golf team. Changing clubs would be a risk. She would need a substantial sum of money to switch clubs and balls."

Chipper came back over near the phone and was vigorously shaking his head back and forth. Stein didn't know much about golf, really, and Chipper didn't want Cindy changing clubs. He had specifically fitted her with the Callaway set, and he didn't want her changing. He whispered to Richard, "Don't do this, Richard. Don't mess around."

Stein said into the phone, "Look, I have to go now, other business to do. If Titleist wants to make an offer for Cindy to use Titleist clubs and balls, then call me. It would have to be at least three million a year. You think about it and call me tomorrow." Then he hung up and turned to Chipper and said, "Crazy. Just absolutely crazy. Tell me about your honeymoon, Chipper."

Chipper animatedly replied, "We had a wonderful honeymoon. We played Anstruther several times. We played the Old Course at St. Andrews three times. The weather cooperated most of the time, even though this is the coldest time of the year. We got to play some of the courses I have always wanted to play; Cruden Bay, Turnberry, Prestwick, Dornoch in the way-up north, Inverness, Muirfield, North Berwick, Gullane number two, Kingsbarns, Carnoustie. I absolutely love the old-style courses, North Berwick is the most fun to play. Cruden Bay is incredible. Prestwick is fun. We had a great time."

"What about the sex, Chipper?" Stein asked eagerly.

"Look, Richard. I don't have any more time to waste. I have to get over to Spanish Bay. You, I'm sure, are aware that I have been banished to there until the tournament is over. It's my plight, but I came over here to find out if you know anything about the house next to mine that apparently has some new people living in it. They've got some vicious dogs out back, and there seems to be a lot of strange men living in the house."

"I know about your banishment, but Stevens said you get to work with Gil Hanse on the re-doing of the golf course. That should be interesting. I have no idea about the house next to you. Why don't you just go over there and ask them? That seems to be the neighborly thing to do."

"I'm not much of a neighborly guy, Richard. I think you know that. The dogs are a threat to Angus, I think. Very mean-looking dogs. We already had an incident. How do we find out about the house and who is living there?"

"Just go over and ask them, Chipper."

"I won't do that."

Stein finally said, "Let's go for a ride, then. We'll go to Tom Wallen's office. He knows everything going on with property in the Forest."

TOM WALLEN

Chipper and Stein headed outside. Chipper expected to just walk across the putting green to the only real estate office inside the Forest. That didn't happen. Stein's yellow Lexus was parked nearby and Stein walked toward it with Chipper beside. Chipper said, "Why don't we just go across the putting green to the Coldwell Banker office? I don't have time to go anywhere, Richard. Isn't Wallen's office right here?"

"Not any more. He's over in Carmel near 5th and Junipero. We'll take a quick drive over there and talk to him."

"It will take too much time, Richard. I don't have the time. I actually want to get off to a good start over at Spanish Bay."

Stein beckoned for Chipper to get in the passenger side of the bright yellow Lexus, and Chipper reluctantly complied. Luckily, Stein drove very fast, evidently not afraid of getting a ticket or tipping the car over on windy roads in the Forest. It was a thrill ride. Of course, there was no parking near the Coldwell Banker office, so Stein just parked in the red zone that was nearest. Stein placed a big placard on his dash board that merely said, STEIN, VICE PRESIDENT, PEBBLE BEACH COMPANY.

The office was large with several agents at desks, most on their cell phones. Several waved at Richard as he entered and walked to a glass enclosed private office in the back. Wallen was there, also on his cell phone. Richard sat down and waited, while Chipper paced back and forth, from wall to wall, in the small enclosure. Wallen was talking too long, and Chipper showed his impatience. Wallen ignored him. Chipper said loudly, "Richard. I really have to go. I don't have time for this." Wallen held up one finger, and Chipper had no idea what that meant. Wallen was on the phone for another few minutes telling whoever was on the other end that his client would not accept any offer under twenty-five million for whatever property he was selling.

Wallen finally said, "What can I do for you, Richard? Do you have a client for me or another abandoned property?"

Stein said, "This is my friend, Chipper Blair. He inherited Ben Morris' estate off the fourteenth fairway at Pebble Beach last year. He has a question for you."

Wallen stood up, "I know you then, Mr. Blair. There was some controversy over your inheritance. Big story. You are one lucky man. It seems you have been in some trouble frequently lately. Do you want to sell your property? You have come to the right place. It's probably worth forty million dollars or more. No problem to sell."

Chipper ignored Wallen's comments and just replied, "I have a question about the property next door to mine. On the side closer to the fourteenth green. We were away for a few weeks, and it seems the house now has new people living in it. Did it sell? They have some vicious dogs in their yard."

Wallen commented, "Why don't you just go over and knock on the door and find out who they are?"

"I'm not very neighborly, and I'm already suspicious about them. Lot of men there in suits, four vicious dogs that we've seen. I hope there are not more. Our friend who came by our house when we were gone says she saw a bunch of men with prayer rugs in the back yard one day."

"Don't judge people by their prayer rugs, Mr. Blair."

"Mr. Wallen. I don't have much time today. I can come back, and we can talk as much as you wish at another time, but just not today. Richard said you know absolutely everything about property ownership in the Forest. If you know about this property, then please tell me."

Wallen started, "It was an interesting case, actually. The owner had no intention of selling, but a man showed up at their door with literally a suitcase full of cash. I sold them the property originally, and it's a bit smaller than your house. Probably worth between thirty-two and thirty-five million. When the man offered them seventy-five million in cash right there on the spot, they called me immediately. Highly unusual, surprising, even in the Forest. I drove right over with some contracts. The man was Arab-looking, but he said his name was Todd Whitebread..."

When Wallen said Whitebread, Stein interrupted, made some sort of strange gasping noises, and said loudly, "That's the same guy who rented my new house. We haven't even moved in yet. He gave me a million for just a month."

Wallen continued, "I handled the transaction and didn't take much commission. Highly unusual indeed. Whitebread turns out to be a representative of the Saudi Public Investment Fund. The house is under ownership of the Sovereign Wealth Fund they operate, but we had to do the paperwork under Whitebread's name. Highly unusual. What a windfall for the homeowners."

Stein said, "Shouldn't we contact the local police about this?"

Wallen commented again, "Don't judge people by their prayer rugs, Richard."

"Well, I'm certainly going to bring it up at our next management meeting in the morning. Maybe I'll go over there myself and see what they are up to. I think I'll drive over there right now."

Chipper was getting impatient, "Not now, Richard. Just take me back to your office, so I can get going. You can go over after and tell me what's up."

24

After they left, Wallen stood up, walked to a photo of Carmel Beach on his wall, and slanted it to the side. He unlocked a safe behind it, just to make sure his commission money of two million in cash was still in there. He said softly to himself, "Highly unusual."

THE LINKS AT SPANISH BAY

Stein dropped off Chipper and then headed to the estate off the fourteenth fairway. Chipper literally jumped in his golf cart and headed toward the Links at Spanish Bay on the heavily tourist travelled Seventeen Mile Drive. He just drove on main roads with many cars honking their horns behind him. He tried to move to the right side of the road on the shoulder. Some of the time he could do that, and other times, he just smiled as the cars made noises behind him. *Stop and smell the flowers and enjoy the Forest,* he thought to himself. This was not a location to be in a hurry.

When he arrived at the pro shop area, he just parked his cart on the path outside the main entrance and left it there. He didn't think he would be there very long. He entered the wood-paneled, very orderly pro shop, and immediately thought that this was a better-organized operation than Spyglass Hill. It was an impressive pro shop area with more impressive prices for golf merchandise and clothes. He glanced at the prices, and they were actually a bit higher than he expected. There weren't too many golfers in the pro shop.

The window behind the cash registers was open to the first tee of the golf course, with the Pacific Ocean in the distance, and extended the whole length of the pro shop. Even Chipper was impressed. There were three identically-dressed attendants waiting patiently for customers and golfers. They were wearing striped golf shirts and sweater vests with the

Spanish Bay logo. The logo was a bagpiper. The course and bar nearby were known for having a bagpiper play at sunset every night. It had become a huge tourist attraction and helped the outside bar seating area have huge sales.

Chipper was looking for assistant pro Jeff Pace and assumed one of the three would be Pace. He went up to the counter and said, "Are one of you Jeff Pace?" All three laughed at the same time, and the identical young man on the left said, "Jeff doesn't work the counter. He comes and goes. If you wait a few minutes, he'll probably show up. Who are you?"

"I'm one of the assistant pros at Pebble, and I'm assigned here for a few weeks."

"You must be Chipper," the one in the middle said. "We have heard about you. It's a pleasure to meet you. I'd love to see your house. I've heard about it. I follow a friend of yours, Cindy Springer, and your new wife on Instagram."

Chipper ignored him and said, "I'll go outside and enjoy the view. It would be great if you told Mr. Pace that I'm waiting outside. Thank you."

It was truly a beautiful setting. Chipper watched a foursome tee off. The first fairway was very wide and had gorgeous views off to the right. Chipper thought to himself, *The first hole would be much better if it headed straight downhill toward the water rather than parallel. I'll have to recommend that to Hanse when I see him.*

Pace came out wearing the same outfit as his three minions inside the pro shop and introduced himself to Chipper. "I think we've met once before somewhere. You look very familiar. Maybe I saw your picture in the newspaper? I was expecting you a few hours ago."

Chipper remained silent, and Pace continued, "Well, I'm glad to have you here, even if it's only for a few weeks. My instructions were to give you something that you couldn't possibly screw up. That you couldn't get in any trouble doing."

"Nice to know I am so well recommended. If you had a driving range, I would love to do that, but you don't. That will be another thing I'll recommend to Gil Hanse."

Pace was surprised, "When will you see Hanse? No one told me you were supposed to talk to Hanse. I'd rather you didn't. He's here today, actually. This is the sixth time he and his team have been over here. They are pretty far along in their planning. They are going to start the renovation as soon as they are done with another project."

"Where is he now?"

"He and three other guys headed out about an hour ago. I let them do what they want. Not sure where they are. Let me tell you what the plan is with you. See the first tee, right there?"

"Obviously I do."

"I've got a guy that stands on the first tee and greets golfers and checks their receipts. He likes to do it from sun-up to about eight forty-five. So I need you to stand on the first tee and check receipts to make sure they paid and just to be nice to them. Make sure they feel they are in a special place and they are our guests. Can you do that? Start at eight forty-five every day, even weekends, and stay until three PM. I've got another guy for the after three PM crowd. When it rains, we'll put up a tent for you for protection. It gets cold and windy out here. What size are you? Medium?"

"Yes."

"We'll have a striped shirt and logo vest, as well as a logo windbreaker for you in the morning. Just wear the same clothes every day. We'll get you a cap and a head warmer cap, as well. What do you want your name tag to say?"

"Chipper would be great. At Spyglass, the pro insisted it say Walter Blair Jr. only. Chipper would be ideal. Thank you."

"You got it, Chipper. Why don't you go out there now and just observe the old guy doing it now. See how he acts and what comments he makes.

Then we'll see you in the morning before eight forty-five. Let's have a hassle-free few weeks."

Chipper said, "I got it, Jeff. Can I hit a few balls from the first tee if there is no one around during the day? I'd like to keep loose and my golf swing in some kind of shape, if I am there for six hours every day."

Pace thought about it, then reluctantly agreed, "But you can't leave the tee to go out there and get the golf balls."

Chipper agreed. "See you in the morning, Mr. Pace. Looking forward to it. After I observe on the first tee, I'm going to head out and try to find Gil Hanse."

GIL HANSE

Chipper had no idea where on the golf course to go. He drove the short distance to the eighteenth green and waited for a group to finish. He asked them if they had seen a few men in golf carts with equipment of some kind on the golf course. They said no, so Chipper figured they weren't on the back nine. He then headed his cart out in the direction of the first hole, hoping to find the noted golf architect and his team. He found them on the par three, fourth hole, named Shepherd's Haven. Their two carts were parked behind the green, in the grass, off the cart path. Four men were walking around on the green, each in a different direction. They all were carrying laptops and looked very involved.

Chipper hopped out of his cart and approached the man he knew was Gil Hanse. Hanse was concentrating and preoccupied and didn't even see Chipper approach. When Chipper reached out his hand and said, "Hello, Mr. Hanse," Hanse was startled.

Hanse shook Chipper's hand and said, "And who might you be?"

"Chipper Blair. I'm an assistant pro at Pebble Beach. I was assigned to Spanish Bay for the next several weeks, and Mr. Stevens said I should help you and your team."

Hanse was polite but said, "News to me. Donald never said anything about that to me. We've been here six times. I don't think we need any help. Are you a golf architect? Had any experience in course design?"

"No I haven't. I'm surprised he didn't say anything to you. He told me he did. I think he admires my knowledge of golf and golf courses."

"Well, I'm surprised he just didn't let you do the renovation then!" Hanse said abruptly. He was no longer trying to be polite. "I'm not sure what you can add to help us."

The other three men walked over, and Hanse said, "Jim, Shaymus, and Tommy, this is Chipper Blair. He's an assistant pro here, and he says Donald has told him to help us. Chipper, this is Jim Wagner, my partner for the last thirty years in our golf course design company. This is Shaymus Maley. I consider Shaymus to be the best course shaper in the business. This is design associate Tommy Naccarato, also one of the best." All four now had big smiles on their faces, not quite laughing but close.

Wagner said, "OK, Chipper. Let's stand behind the green and watch this group on the tee hit up, and you can tell us what you think about the Links at Spanish Bay that you think might help us." At this point all four started laughing. Chipper debated quickly whether to just take off in his cart and forget this, or to try to impress them with his opinions.

"How long have you got?" Chipper asked.

Hanse said, "Take as long as you want."

Chipper started, "First of all, the hole names are stupid here. Spyglass names are all in the same Treasure Island theme. Here they are just silly. To the Sea. Straight and Narrow, Pitch and Run. Why not just say Hard Hole, Easy Hole? Left Begone. Ridiculous. White Dune. Dune Hollow, Sandy. Equally ridiculous." Chipper looked at the four faces and saw no reaction.

"The course is called The Links at Spanish Bay, but it is not really an authentic links course. It has too many elevated greens. Too many tree-lined holes in the middle. Tatum and Watson really weren't architects.

Jones shouldn't have taken their opinions on anything. He would have done a much better job of routing without them."

Chipper noticed that Naccarato actually started typing a few things into his laptop.

"There are too many forced layups and doglegs. Too many in-course out of bounds. Everyone hates in-course out of bounds. I know the dunes are environmentally protected, but I'm sure General Counsel Stein can figure some way around that. He's very resourceful. I imagine you have talked to him about that?"

This time Wagner typed something on his laptop.

"It is recognized as the weakest course in the Pebble Beach Company collection. The greens are often lumpy and slow. It's too windy. There is no driving range here. Who ever played on a great course with no driving range? Ludicrous. The routing has most holes going parallel to Spanish Bay. Sure you can look right or left and see the water, but there should be some holes that go straight at the water. You've been here six times; tell me are there any truly memorable holes out here? I've played here several times, have a great memory for great holes, and I can't remember any hole except number one. And that's because I just looked at it. Nothing is memorable. Make some truly great memorable holes."

Now all three were furiously typing.

"How about making some double greens like at St. Andrews? How about a short par three, like the seventh at Pebble? How about holes where you can hit driver comfortably. There is too much mounding in the wrong places. The greens are too big. Should I go on?"

Hanse just nodded his head indicating yes.

Chipper looked at the four golfers now on the green and said, "Ask them what they think so far about the course. Are they getting their three hundred and forty dollar green fees worth? And their sixty dollar cart fee worth?

All four went over to the four men around the pin, and Chipper asked them his questions.

They were reluctant to start, but when they did, their opinions flowed right after the other, "The greens are lumpy. I'm surprised the course isn't in better shape. I hit a drive just off the fairway on one hole, and the sign said I couldn't go get it. It was out of bounds. I could see it, so I went into the protected dunes and just played it anyway. Silly rules. Too many forced lay ups so far. The course marshal who drove by was unpleasant. Hard to play the ninety-degree cart path rule. Some holes have cart paths, and some don't. Why not just eliminate the cart paths? It's supposed to be a links course."

Chipper finally had to say, "That's enough, fellows. Enjoy your golf. Sorry to hold you up." None of the four golfers recognized Gil Hanse.

Chipper asked, "Have you guys played the course or just walked around six times?"

Hanse said, "Of course, we have played. Some of your stuff is good stuff, most of it we recognized already. How about we show you our new course maps and ideas in a few days? I think you'll enjoy them. I'd love to have your opinion on a few things, actually. I'll tell Donald that we appreciate your input. Glad to have met you."

Chipper said, "I'm here on the first tee now from eight forty-five AM until three in the afternoon for the next three weeks. Every day. Just come get me when you want to meet with me or ask me any questions."

Chipper headed back toward the 17-Mile Drive and his estate.

IRENE MCVAY

Irene McVay took a very long time deciding what to wear that late afternoon. It was just before sunset. She was a very attractive fifty-nine-year-old woman who lived in a large estate off the eleventh hole at Pebble Beach Golf Course. After Chipper stopped living in her guest house, she was reluctant to rent it to another young man. Her relationship with Big Bill O'Shea was going extremely well, and he was sleeping at her estate three times a week. She was sleeping at his house a few times a week. She certainly didn't need the money from the rental, but she felt her life lacked the excitement she felt when Chipper was in the guest house. She craved attention, and Chipper couldn't resist her. He was moneyless then, and the lower rental rate he paid was for services that both Chipper and Irene enjoyed.

She had finally decided, against Big Bill's protestations, to rent to a Monterey Institute of International Studies student. For some reason he was looking for a rental in Pebble Beach, although it was not convenient to the main campus in downtown Monterey. When she interviewed him, he said that he loved the idea of living in the Forest. He moved in the following week after the interview. Unlike in Chipper's situation, she didn't mention the services necessary to get lower rent. He paid full price with cash: first, last, and a deposit. He looked Arab or Middle Eastern, but his name was Greg Whitebread. Greg had been in the guest house for several days, and all she knew was that he was picked up each morning in a black sedan, and he always wore a black suit and tie.

She finished looking in the mirror and liked what she saw. Her legs were still great for a fifty- nine-year-old, and she wore a short skirt to show them off. Her top was low-cut and sleeveless and showed off her toned arms. Her last move was to fluff up her hair, so it came down in wisps on her forehead. She confidently headed out her back door and around to the guest house. When she rounded the corner, she saw Whitebread kneeling toward the east on a prayer rug that was on the small lawn. His head was near the ground. She quietly turned around and went back to her home. She sat in the kitchen with a glass of scotch and googled how long Muslim prayers lasted and decided to go back in twenty minutes. She found that Muslims do Salah prayers five times a day, and they take between ten and fifteen minutes.

She fluffed up her hair again and walked back to the guest house. The yard was empty, and she knocked on the front door. Whitebread answered immediately and politely said, "Hello, Mrs. McVay. Can I help you?" He didn't open the door more than a crack, barely enough to put his head in the opening. She noticed he had piercing black eyes and took a few seconds to say anything.

"Hello, Greg. It is Greg, isn't it? I would like to have a conversation with you about a few things. We really don't know each other very well, and I'd like to learn more about you. I always become friends with my tenants. We haven't talked yet, really, other than the initial interview. Can I come in? Is this a good time?"

Whitebread said, "Not really a good time, Mrs. McVay. I have an appointment soon and have to clean up."

She was surprised that he was staring only into her eyes and his head didn't move up and down to look at her outfit. Most young men, even though she was almost sixty, would have given her the "once over." She said, "Oh. That's too bad. Can I come over and talk tomorrow then? Is there a good time?"

"Tomorrow won't work, unless it's early in the morning. I have to go to class at eight."

"I'm up early," Irene said, "What if I come over at seven, and we chat a bit? I'll bring you a cup of coffee and a scone."

Irene could tell Whitebread was reluctant, but he politely said, "I don't drink regular coffee. If you have decaf, that would be good. And I am watching my weight, so I don't need a treat. It is nice of you to offer. I'll come over to your house and knock on the back door when I am ready in the morning, if that is OK."

"That's fine. Thank you. It will be nice to chat a bit."

He said, "Can I ask you to cover your arms and legs when I come over? I know it seems strange, but I would feel more comfortable if you did that. I am sorry to ask, but it would make me much more comfortable. Thank you."

"OK. See you about seven then, Mr. Whitebread. Can I call you Greg?"

"That is my name. Certainly. See you in the morning." Then he closed the door.

Irene decided she would have to use her guest house key to examine the room tomorrow when he was gone. The conversation certainly didn't go as she planned.

CHIPPER'S PLANS

When Jenny returned home in the early evening, she found Chipper in the study bending over maps of the Del Monte Forest. He was so engrossed and concentrating that he didn't hear her come up behind him. She debated whether to say something or just purposely startle him by hugging him from behind. She tiptoed up quietly, but Angus cut her short by barking when she got a few steps behind. Chipper turned to see Angus and saw Jenny instead. They hugged like they had not seen each other for weeks. "I missed you today, Chipper."

"And I missed you, too." He was surprised how much he actually did miss her and didn't release the hug for a long time. And only reluctantly when Angus got impatient.

Jenny said, "What are you doing, Mr. Chips?"

"Today went really well," he said, "I was told one of my new duties at Spanish Bay was to help the golf course architect, Gil Hanse, in his renovation of the golf course. My conversation with Hanse and his team went better than I expected. Of course, they weren't expecting me. Stevens never said anything to them. They were almost laughing at first, but by the end of my reasons for not liking Spanish Bay, they were all taking notes. They want to show me their plans. That's a big deal, I think."

Jenny said, "Good stuff. Let's hug again." And they did, until Angus got uncomfortable. "What are you doing with those maps?"

"This is really cool. Let me show you." He picked up his notes on the table. "I am relegated to first tee greeter and checking golf receipts for the next three weeks. I have to work from eight forty-five to three PM. Listen to this. You are going to love this. I figure I can leave early and play my way into work over there. This is great. I leave here early, after the morning shot, and go back to the tee on fourteen. I play fourteen and fifteen at Pebble, then cut over to the 17-Mile Drive road. I go by the Hay on Stevenson over to Spyglass and play holes ten, eleven, twelve, and thirteen. Then I cut through the trees over to Forest Lake and take that to Lopez over to Bird Rock Road. Then back to a left on Stevenson again, and I play holes five, six, seven, and eight at the Monterey Peninsula Country Club shore course."

Jenny was laughing at this point and trying to follow along on the maps spread out on the table. She said, "MPCC is private."

Chipper said, "I know that, Jenny. Did you know membership there is now four hundred and fifty thousand dollars, and dues are two thousand a month? And there is a waiting list! For me, a drop in the bucket, but why do people do that? It will be early. I'm sure no one will hassle me."

Jenny commented, "It will be dark in the morning. How are you going to handle that?"

"Let me finish. I have that all figured out, too. No problem. Let me finish my morning route. After the eighth hole on the shore course, I head out to the 17-Mile Drive again over to Spanish Bay Road and Spanish Bay Drive. I jump on at hole ten, then after the eleventh, I see what time it is and decide if I should just drive to the Pro Shop and first tee, or I have time to play twelve, thirteen, fourteen, and fifteen, and then to the Pro Shop. This is so great. I'm gonna love the next three weeks. And I get off at three. We can go play Cypress after that. I'm a lucky man." He hugged Jenny again.

Jenny said, "How are you going to see in the morning?"

He took her by the hand, and they walked down the hall to get to the deck off the kitchen. In the kitchen, he picked up a piece of equipment that looked like a big flashlight on the table.

"What the heck is that?" Jenny asked.

"You'll see," Chipper replied, "Wait until we get outside in the dark."

When they were on the deck, Chipper turned on the flashlight-looking piece of equipment, and he said, "Don't look at it directly." Jenny was amazed as it lit up the entire area across the fourteenth fairway. Chipper clicked a button, and it was even brighter, illuminating an area Jenny guessed was one hundred yards wide.

Chipper said, "I drove into the military surplus store in Seaside after work. What we have here is a tactical flashlight. Almost a million lumens. It's LED and rechargeable. Works eight hours without a charge on regular mode and two hours at this mode I have it on now. It goes out two hundred and forty yards. It's even water resistant."

Jenny said, "It makes it look like daylight out there."

"That's the idea, my beautiful wife."

"You are crazy, my handsome husband."

"I'm looking forward to the next three weeks now, exciting," Chipper whispered.

"Just stay out of trouble, Chipper."

"How could I possibly get in any trouble on the first tee at Spanish Bay?"

RICHARD STEIN

A bit later in the evening, Chipper took a phone call from Richard Stein. Stein was excited.

"Hi, Chipper. After I dropped you off, I went right to the estate next to yours and rang the intercom at the gate in front. No one answered. I parked across the street for about twenty minutes and just watched. Several black Escalades came to the gate in kind of a caravan. I couldn't see inside, because the windows were all tinted. I stopped counting at seven. There were probably ten or eleven. When they were all in and the gate closed, I waited a few minutes, then drove back to the gate and tried the intercom again. No one answered again. I drove back across the street and called the Seaside Cadillac dealer to see if they would tell me if they rented any Escalades out lately. I was surprised when the manager told me about six months back, they received an order for twenty-three black Escalades from a guy named Whitebread. He paid cash in advance. Do you know they cost about one hundred and twenty thousand each?"

"What are you going to do, Richard?" asked Chipper.

"Let me finish my story first. I left and drove to Emily Hastings' house. I guess I should say my estate. Isn't that amazing? It's going to take a while to make it mine and feel comfortable saying that. When I got to the front gate of MY estate, I used the code, and it didn't work. Can you imagine that? They changed the gate code on MY gate. My estate gate!

What a nerve. I don't have a number for Whitebread. Can't even call to see what is going on. I'm going to call our friends, Deputies Anderson and Henderson, and Assistant D.A. Sloane, and see what I can do. I want to get in there and inspect. It's my estate. This is all very fishy now. I'm getting worried."

"What can I do, Richard? I don't want to create any waves during the ATT tournament."

"Since when did Chipper Blair not want to create any waves? Just go over there and introduce yourself as the neighbor, and see if you can look around. Be neighborly."

"I don't think I'll do that, Richard. Maybe Irene might go over there and play the inquisitive old lady in the neighborhood."

"I don't think she would like you to call her an old lady. That's evident. But, yes, I think that is a good idea. Go ahead and ask her."

DOG DANGER

The next morning Chipper and Jenny were up very early. Angus slept in between them, but it didn't keep them from making love twice. The first time Angus watched, but he was asleep or bored for the second time. When they walked down the back steps, Angus was again reluctant to descend. Jenny had to pick him up and carry him to the lawn. It was cold and damp. Neither Jenny nor Chipper could hear any dogs barking in the estate next door. Angus seemed to sense them, as he huddled near Chipper's legs when Jenny hit her morning shot.

She knew it was a good one the moment it left the club head. Angus was reluctant to take off, but Chipper coaxed him into heading toward the fourteenth green. Jenny ran up the stairs and was eager to see how close the ball was to the pin. It was too dark to see. Chipper tried his tactical flashlight on high, and it lit up the whole area. He thought to himself, *"Why didn't I get one of these a long time ago?"* After Jenny yelled down that her ball was only a few feet away from the cup, Chipper pointed the beam of light toward the back yard next door. He saw the five dogs waiting silently near the end of the yard. Chipper hoped the electric fence was on.

Angus picked up the ball and headed back down the fairway and not his usual route back near the neighbors estate. When Angus was even with the house, the dogs started a frenzied barking. Chipper still had the flashlight pointed toward them. He saw several lights go on in the estate windows. The five dogs started moving toward where Angus was running and immediately started yelping as they hit the electrified area. One of them, a Pit bull, had gained enough momentum, however, that he or she was through the electrified barrier. The dog was yelping in pain and rolling on the ground but recovered quickly and made a beeline toward where Angus was running.

Chipper immediately started running with his flashlight in one hand and the long spoon golf club in the other. He ran toward the spot he estimated the Pit bull would intercept Angus. Luckily, he got there first, and as the Pit bull approached, Angus darted out toward the middle of the fourteenth fairway. Chipper swung his long spoon at the dog and tried to knock his legs out from under him. He managed to hit one of the legs and the dog yelped but didn't fall. Jenny was yelling from the deck. All the lights in the estate next door came on, and some men came running out to the back yard.

Chipper swung again and this time hit both front legs of the charging dog. The dog yelped in pain again and went down to the ground. Chipper was worried he would hurt the golf club but he aimed right at the top of the dog's head and hit him solidly. The Pit bull, although angered and whimpering, was stunned. When the dog got up, he limped back toward the estate. The men in the back yard were yelling in a foreign language, and Chipper couldn't understand what they were saying. When Angus saw the other dog limping back, he hurried to the back steps and ran up to Jenny. Jenny again picked him up and hugged him.

The Pit bull approached the end of the yard slowly and completely forgot the electrified area would again agitate him. When he got zapped again, there was again furious yelling from the men in the foreign tongue. Jenny took Angus inside, as she figured they would now turn off the electrified field.

Chipper yelled to them, "Keep those dogs inside your property!"

There was a yell back in English, "You'll pay for this! Keep that little black dog away from here! And don't hurt our dogs! You'll pay!" Then he heard someone say to the Pit bull. "You stupid dog."

Chipper went up the stairs and made sure Jenny and Angus were OK before he went back to the lawn and hit his morning shot. He knew he was going to have to hurry and maybe skip some holes in order to get to work on time. He was also afraid that the other four dogs might be on the loose as he drove his cart toward the green. He replaced the long spoon in the backyard cabinet and grabbed a pitching wedge to carry while he was driving to the fourteenth green to retrieve the Slazenger.

He got no more than fifty yards when one of the Dobermans ran toward his cart. Chipper quickly shined the tactical flashlight on laser beam into the dog's eyes. The dog was disoriented immediately, and Chipper slowed his cart down and took a swing similar to what a polo player would do from a horse with his wedge. He clobbered the Doberman in the neck and the dog went down in a heap. Chipper was happy to only see one dog, and he didn't care if the Doberman ever got up again. He heard the men yelling again but was far enough away that he couldn't tell what they said.

He was shaking when he picked up his Slazenger on the fourteenth green and walked to the fifteenth tee. He shined his almost one million lumens out toward the fairway and put it on the ground next to him while he took several deep breaths and hit a great drive down the middle. It was almost like daylight. He lost the ball's flight when it approached what he knew was the two hundred and forty yard visible area of light. *This is great,* he thought to himself, as he took some calming breaths and headed down the cart path to the left of the fairway.

Chipper's flashlight beam worked great. When he turned it on, daylight appeared in the fairways he played that morning. He only needed it on hole fifteen at Pebble and holes ten through twelve at Spyglass. By the time he was on thirteen at Spyglass, it was light enough that he didn't need it. When he illuminated some of the holes he played, he saw home lights come on just off the fairways. It didn't bother him.

PEBBLE BEACH COMPANY MORNING MEETING

CEO Donald Stevens started that morning's meeting by saying, "We had several complaint phone calls this morning by residents at Pebble and Spyglass about very bright lights coming from the golf courses near their homes. So bright that it alarmed them. Did anyone here have maintenance assigned to do work this morning?"

No one answered. Stevens continued, "Very strange. I wonder what is going on. The complaints came from four different calls a bit before seven this morning. We'll have to see if we get any more complaints. I know I was not aware of any course work going on early."

The Director of Golf Operations said, "The courses are in great shape now. We could start the ATT tournament now. We just have to do regular maintenance and let the rough grow just a bit more. We don't want it U.S. Open length. We want them to score pretty well and not be too penal. The grass is pristine on both courses."

Stevens said, "I actually got a compliment about Blair yesterday late from Gil Hanse. I think it's the first time I've ever heard anything good about him. Hanse said he gave his group some good opinions on the Spanish Bay redo. I couldn't believe it. Good idea to get him out of the main tournament area and over there."

Roger Hennessey said, "He's a very knowledgeable guy, Donald.

Knows a lot about golf and golf courses. You should sit down and talk to him some day."

"No thanks, Roger. He's just been a pain in my ass for as long as he's been here. I just hope he stays out of trouble over at Spanish Bay."

Richard Stein asked, "Does anyone here know anything about the Saudi presence that started last week. They bought an estate off the fourteenth fairway at Pebble. There are a lot of them staying there. All driving black Escalades. There are another bunch in my estate, renting for a few weeks. They also have a bunch of Escalades. They changed my gate code, and I can't get in. Can we send security over to both houses to see what's up? I've already got calls in to the county sheriff's office and the D.A.'s office about them."

The Director of Golf Operations commented, "The PGA rep told me that there might be some LIV representatives here during ATT week to observe how we run a Signature Event. None of them have contacted me directly, but they may be part of the LIV group or the Saudi Investment fund group. The PGA and LIV still haven't formalized any structure of the supposed merger."

Stevens commented, "I'll send Jose from our security team over to both houses, Richard. I'd like to know what they are doing, too. You would think that someone from such a large group would give me a courtesy call. I'll follow up with that after out meeting. Thanks for alerting me. Keep me posted on what the sheriff's office and D.A.'s office do."

FIRST TEE

Chipper didn't get to play the last four holes, as planned, at Spanish Bay. Because of the dog incidents earlier, he was late, and had to drive straight to the pro shop after he played the tenth and eleventh holes. He found his striped shirt, name tag, logo vest, and windbreaker waiting for him and dressed quickly. He was happy the name tag just said 'Chipper' rather than Walter Blair, Jr. He replaced the guy on the first tee five minutes early. It was colder, windier, and foggier at the Spanish Bay first tee than it was even a few hours earlier when he started at Pebble Beach.

The first foursome that came to the first tee were the first of three groups from some tech company from the Silicon Valley that was having an outing. They were all young, Chipper guessed under thirty, and looked like golfers. He checked their receipts and waited until the group ahead was out of range before he gave them the OK to tee off. He heard them chatting about their free rooms, care of their company, from the night before. One guy had an ocean view room and the rate listed on the door of the room was sixteen hundred and forty-five dollars a night. One guy was surprised he had a suite that went for thirty-two hundred a night. The two employees kidded each other about why one had a suite and the other didn't.

When he watched them tee off, he was impressed with two of them, but two were hacks. One guy hit so far to the right that Chipper commented, "You better hit another one. That one is never going to be found."

The young guy turned around and said, "I'll find it."

Chipper knew better and was ready to comment but uncharacteristically held his comment to himself. He was proud of himself. First group off the tee, and no problems yet.

When the second group was waiting, it looked like the fairway was clear, but Chipper held them up and pointed out with his flashlight that the guy in the dunes to the right was still wandering around aimlessly looking for his golf ball. The four players on the tee all said at the same time, "Stewie will never give up. He probably only brought one golf ball." Chipper laughed along with them.

They all started yelling, "Stewie. Step it up. Just drop one." They were yelling as loud as they could and laughing as well. Chipper was having a good time.

One guy in the third group asked Chipper where he should hit his drive on the very wide fairway. Chipper obliged by shining his tactical light on laser beam to show the golfer exactly what line to take and where to hit the ball. The foursome was impressed immediately, "Never seen anything like that before. What a great idea. Thank you."

Chipper decided the flashlight was the best purchase he had ever made. There was a break between the tech company groups and the next group off, and Chipper used the opportunity to hit two drives down the fairway. He hit two Titleist ProV1s down the middle. He told the next group to just keep the balls he hit down the fairway. Chipper got some great reviews on Yelp that day. Totally unexpected but great. The reviews praised the starter for being fun and providing great service.

IRENE AND GREG WHITEBREAD

Irene McVay waited with some trepidation for a knock on her back door. She wasn't sure her renter, Whitebread, would show up for coffee as he promised. She had worn casual and skin-covering cotton sweatpants with a long-sleeve Nike sweatshirt on the top. She wore a visor and took the additional step of wrapping a scarf around her neck and shoulders. She didn't know how she would impress the young man dressed like she was. She didn't know how to act.

There was a knock on the door at exactly seven AM, not a second before or a second after. She answered immediately and held out her hand. Whitebread nodded his head but didn't return the handshake. She started, "Thank you, Greg. Can I call you Greg?"

"Yes. Greg is fine. Thank you for inviting me to coffee, Mrs. McVay. I don't have a lot of time. I am going to be picked up at seven thirty for class. And can I have decaf please? I don't like to drink a lot of caffeine."

Irene leaned closer and said, "You can call me Irene. I usually become very good friends with my tenants. Very good friends."

Whitebread leaned back uncomfortably. Irene was impressed with his looks. He was very dark skinned, with straight black hair that he parted on the left; the part was maybe a bit higher on his head than normal. He was thin and a bit taller than Chipper but shorter than Big Bill. He stood up very straight. He was dressed in golf clothes, nicely-tailored black slacks and a polo shirt with a logo that Irene did not recognize. He squinted his dark eyes and Irene felt maybe he needed eyeglasses but didn't want to wear them. She noticed some expensive looking rings, one on the middle finger of each hand. They were matching.

"Tell me about yourself, Greg."

"I told you everything when you interviewed me for the guest house. I like it very much. It has a nice garden and view of the garden from the living room. It is very comfortable. I am a student at the Monterey Institute of International Studies. I am in a master's degree program."

"What are you studying?"

"Arab studies. I was born in Saudi Arabia but came to this country when very young. I would like to go back one day." He sipped his decaf.

"Where did you live when you came to the United States?"

"My mother came to Minneapolis and we lived with her sister. My father..." he hesitated, "Well, I never knew my father, really. My mother raised me. She didn't talk at all about my father."

"That's too bad. Looking at you, I am sure he was a very handsome man. Do you have a girlfriend?" Irene leaned in again.

Whitebread looked embarrassed and simply said, "No." He quickly finished his decaf and winced, because it was still very hot.

Irene reached out to touch his face and said, "Poor boy. I'm sorry the decaf is too hot."

He recoiled so much he almost fell off his chair, and Irene laughed.

"You make me uncomfortable, Mrs. McVay. I don't think I've ever met a woman like you. Very uncomfortable. I really have to go. I don't want to miss my ride."

"I am very sorry that I make you uncomfortable. I enjoy getting to know my renters. Are you comfortable with the rent we agreed on, or would you like to make some arrangements with me for cheaper rent?"

"I am very comfortable with the rent. It is more than reasonable. I am lucky that I have no financial issues. I don't think I need any other arrangements to lower my rent. Money is not a big problem. I have a good scholarship."

"Now that we know each other a bit better, we should meet again, Greg, and talk about lowering your rent. We can be friends. I like having a friend on the property. It is a big property."

She walked him out the front door, out her front gate, and waited with him for his ride.

"You don't have to wait with me, Mrs. McVay."

"It's OK, Greg." She reached over and rubbed his lower back. He moved away quickly.

They waited in silence until a black Escalade slowly pulled up and stopped in front of them. Whitebread quickly entered the back seat and said, "Thank you for the coffee, Mrs. McVay."

Irene watched the car drive away. She wasn't happy with her time with Whitebread and a bit suspicious about the Escalade that picked him up each morning. She went back in the house and grabbed a key to her guest house. In the kitchen she put on some rubber gloves, just because she thought it would be a good idea. Although she didn't have to be quiet, she carefully snuck around to her guest house and opened the door.

At first glance, the guest house was pristine, almost like no one was living there. The prayer rug was rolled up and leaning on the wall near the front door. There were no personal items anywhere she could see in the living room: no pictures, no books, no newspapers, no coins. She opened a few drawers carefully, and they were empty. In the small kitchen, there were no dirty dishes or utensils in the sink. She checked the cabinets, and the dishes and glasses all looked unused, as they were before she rented the house out to Whitebread.

In the bedroom, there were no textbooks or papers that she could see. The bathroom had one bottle of cologne near the sink. There was one full bar of soap in the shower. The bedroom closets only had a few pants and shirts, as well as a black suit and tie. Irene checked the top drawer of the nightstand and took out two folded blueprints. She was hoping she could fold them back to how she found them. One was of the Grand Ballroom in the Lodge at Pebble Beach, and the other was of the Grand Ballroom of the Inn at Spanish Bay. She immediately thought she should call someone and decided to start with Richard Stein.

Irene tiptoed out of her guest house, locked the door behind her, took a deep breath, and went back to her kitchen. Her heart was beating very fast. She dialed Stein's office, and after a short pause, he answered, "Richard Stein, General Counsel and Vice President, Pebble Beach Company."

"I'm NOT impressed, Richard. This is Irene McVay."

"You should be," he said, "What can I do for you, Irene? I am a very impressive man, you know."

"I have a new guest house tenant named Greg Whitebread…"

Stein Interrupted, "Greg Whitebread! Really! Very interesting. The person who bought the estate next to Chipper's is named Todd Whitebread, same as the guy who rented my estate for the next three weeks. Lot of Whitebreads. Can't be a coincidence. What does he look like?"

"He's a handsome Arab-looking man. He said he was born in Saudi Arabia but moved to Minnesota when he was very young. He's a student at the Monterey Institute."

"Did you call because you suspect something, Irene?"

"I don't want to be biased just because he is Arab, but I happened to notice in the guest house that he had blueprints of the ballroom at the Lodge and the ballroom at Spanish Bay…"

Stein interrupted again, "Wow. I'm glad you called. Now it sounds suspicious. What we have heard is they are here to observe the ATT golf this year. They are associated with the new LIV golf group and the Saudi Investment Fund."

Irene commented, "The what and the what? You are talking gibberish, Richard."

"Don't you worry, Irene. I'll handle this," Stein said, then abruptly hung up.

SPCA OF
MONTEREY COUNTY

Executive Support Manager, Laura Kelley, of the Monterey County SPCA, started her usual daily review of any online reports of animal cruelty. There were several every day about dogs being kept outside at night and keeping the neighbors up by their continuous barking. She typically ignored those. Many of this type were reported by the same person almost every day.

When she saw a report that the reporter titled, Two Dogs Maimed, she perked up, took a few sips of her coffee, and read it thoroughly twice. She forwarded it to her boss, CEO Scott Delucchi. She also thought it was important enough that she printed it off and walked down the hall to Delucchi's office.

Delucchi was reading the online report when Kelley walked into his office. She took a chair at the side of his desk. He said, "Wow. This is unbelievable. This guy took golf clubs, unprovoked, to two of their dogs. We usually don't have any reports of abuse from Pebble Beach. We have to send an agent over there. Delucchi called his Humane Investigations Supervisor, Jacob Duarte, and told him to come to his office. "They don't have a name for the guy that did it. They just say it's a neighbor," Delucchi continued.

When Duarte came in and took the remaining chair in the small office, Delucchi explained that a complaint from a Bill Whitebread, from a Pebble Beach estate, claimed that his neighbor had pummeled one of his dogs with a golf club, blinded another dog with a laser beam, and used a golf club again to hit the same poor blinded dog on the head. "I'm going to call Whitebread and tell him we are sending over an investigator now. Can you head over there now, Jacob? This is a serious one."

Delucchi put the phone on speaker and called the number in the report. Laura Kelley handed the printed report to Duarte. When the phone was answered, Delucchi said, "Hello, is Mr. Whitebread there?"

"Which Mr. Whitebread?" the foreign-sounding voice on the other end answered. "Who is this calling?"

"Bill Whitebread. This is Scott Delucchi, with the SPCA of Monterey County, following up on an animal abuse report."

"I will get him," said the foreign voice. Before Bill Whitebread came on the phone, he heard the man who answered the phone say, in the background, "I told you not to report this. We don't want any attention brought on us. You are an idiot."

Bill said, "Hello, this is Bill Whitebread. Who is this?"

Delucchi again said, "This is Scott Delucchi, CEO of the SPCA, following up on your report of very serious dog abuse. I have two others from my staff listening. I have you on the speaker phone." Delucchi noticed that Whitebread had no accent. "Thank you for reporting this abuse. We want to send out our Supervisor of Investigations to talk to you and see the dogs."

"Can't you just go visit the neighbor who did this? A horrible man, obviously."

"We would like to talk to you and see the dogs before we go visit him. I hope your dogs are OK. Did you take them to the veterinarian? Which one?"

"The dogs were in pain. One could barely walk. We had them put away already."

"Really. Which vet did that?"

"They were in so much pain, we had to do it ourselves."

Delucchi heard the foreign voice in the background say loudly, "Holy fuck, Jamal. Watch what you say."

"I hope you put them away humanely."

"It was very quick. They felt no pain."

The voice in the back again said, "Get off the phone, Jamal. I told you not to report this. We can handle this ourselves."

"Tell me about this incident please, Mr. Whitebread," said Delucchi.

"Our dogs were playing in our back yard, just before dawn, when this vicious little black dog from the neighbor's yard, started barking at our peaceful dogs. Our peaceful dogs wandered over, and for some reason, the next door neighbor, who was strangely out before dawn hitting golf balls, walked over and viciously attacked our dogs with his golf clubs and with some sort of laser beam he was carrying."

"Do you know his name?"

"I did not when I filed the report, but I found out this morning his name is Walter Blair. He lives in the estate next door to ours. We are new to the neighborhood. We never expected such a terrifying experience for our peaceful dogs."

"Did you report this to anyone else?"

"I did. I tried every resource I could find. I reported it online to the Monterey County Sheriff's Office, the Pebble Beach Community Association, and the Del Monte Forest homeowners association."

"Did you get any other replies back?"

"Not yet."

"I am going to send Mr. Duarte out now to visit you and your neighbor, Mr. Blair, and get to the bottom of this. Will you be home?"

"I am going out, but my friend can meet you in the back yard. You have the address?"

"Yes. You reported it. What is your friend's name?"

"George. Just walk around the house to the back yard, please, when you get here."

"And what is George's last name? Our guy will be there in about forty minutes."

"He goes by Whitebread as well."

Delucchi hung up and said to his employees, "Very strange conversation. Jacob, I want you to take another person with you. In fact, take our vet, Dr. Riley."

JERRY DEVINE

Jerry Devine, the last remaining writer on the staff of the Monterey Herald newspaper, was doing his usual great job of looking at every possible source of news in the area. He combed the county sheriff's reports every morning to look for newsworthy items. When he read the complaint against Chipper Blair for animal abuse, he called Chipper.

"Chipper. Jerry Devine here from the Herald."

"What can I do for you, Jerry? Looking for news? Sorry. I haven't done anything newsworthy lately."

"Really, you have, Chipper. There was a complaint to the sheriff's department that you maimed two dogs. It's from your neighbor."

"You have to be kidding me. They filed a report? I was just protecting Angus. They had a Pit bull and a Doberman who were after Angus, and I kept them away from the poor little dog. Angus was terrified. We've sent him over to Irene's for a while. It's too dangerous at our house. I told her to make sure he gets to chase golf balls every morning. Poor little guy. I can't believe they filed a report."

"Actually, they had to put down the dogs because of the damage you did."

"That's crazy. I tapped one with the long spoon on the legs, and I hit the other one when it came after me with my wedge."

"I have to write it up, Chipper. Can I say you did it in self-defense?"

"You don't have to do this, Jerry. Don't do this, please."

"It's my job to report the news, Chipper. It means more to me than friendship."

"That's obvious to me."

"Can I quote you, then?"

Chipper paused, then finally said, "I have no comment. This is ridiculous."

Devine started writing an online Herald report immediately about the animal abuse report. Blair certainly was newsworthy. He had all the information he needed without even calling Mr. Whitebread, who filed the complaint.

MONTEREY HERALD

BYLINE DEVINE PEBBLE BEACH

DOG ABUSE IN PEBBLE BEACH

How much trouble can one man cause? In the case of Pebble Beach resident, Walter "Chipper" Blair, the answer seems to be unlimited. A serious case of animal abuse was reported to the Monterey County Sheriff's Department yesterday, claiming that Blair maimed two peaceful dogs for no apparent reason. The weapon seemed to be Blair's usual weapons of choice, his golf clubs.

His neighbor, in the very expensive estate area off the fourteenth hole at Pebble Beach Golf Course, a Mr. Whitebread, accuses Mr. Blair of attacking his two dogs early in the morning yesterday. He claims his dogs were in his back yard and Blair clubbed one dog with some type of golf club and then blinded another dog with a laser beam before clubbing the dog on the head. Whitebread says both dogs were maimed and in great pain and had to be put away.

The sheriff's department and the Monterey County SPCA are both investigating the allegations. California Penal Code 597 C specifically says it is a crime to mutilate, torture, or wound or kill a living animal. A finding of guilty is punishable by up to three years in prison and a twenty thousand dollar fine. The SPCA has three sworn officers specifically trained in animal abuse cases. Intentional and malicious abuse is a punishable felony. On the Federal level, animal cruelty and intentional acts can have a punishment of up to seven years in prison.

In a phone conversation, Blair said that the charges are ridiculous. He had no other comments about the allegations.

THE WHITEBREAD ESTATE

It was a busy day at the Whitebread estate. Bill Whitebread has prepared for the visit of the SPCA investigator. The front gate of the estate was left wide open, the electric fence was turned off, the two Dobermans and one Pit bull had been drugged with some Valium in their food. The others in the house made sure they drove all the black Escalades away before the SPCA personnel arrived. Whitebread wasn't sure the human Valium dose would work, so he locked the three dogs in one of the house's downstairs bedrooms. He hoped, perhaps, the investigator would only ask questions about the incident and wouldn't want to see the remaining three dogs.

Whitebread was apprehensive, because he had been chastised for bringing attention to their estate. He wanted this to go very well, and the next-door neighbor to be punished badly.

Jacob Duarte and Dr. Kate Riley drove through the front gate and parked. As instructed earlier, they didn't knock on the front door but took the pathway around the house to the back yard. Bill Whitebread was waiting.

Duarte said, "I am Jacob Duarte, the primary humane investigations officer. This is Dr. Kate Riley, our SPCA Chief Veterinarian. Beautiful house and back yard, right on the golf course. This view is amazing. How long have you been in the house?"

Whitebread tried to make all his answers short and to the point, "Just three weeks."

Duarte said, "Can I call you Mr. Whitebread or Jamal? I think I heard that name on the phone call."

"No one here named Jamal. My name is Bill. I did the report. It was a horrible atrocity. What is the crazy man next door doing out in the dark hitting golf balls so early in the morning? And his dog was vicious."

"Tell me about it. Did you see it? All of it?"

"Not really. One of the other people that lives here saw it all."

"We would like to talk to that person then, right now. Can you go get him or her?"

"They are at work now. He told me about the incident in a very detailed way. I can show you exactly what happened."

"Go ahead and do that," said Duarte, who gestured with his hands toward Chipper's estate next door.

Whitebread mimicked his gesture and said, "Our five dogs were in the back yard because we let them out every morning to do their thing, after being inside all night. They were roaming the back yard when this black dog from next door walked up to our yard and started tormenting the dogs by barking. I explained everything in the online report, you know. One of our dogs walked over peacefully to the black dog, and the black dog ran away toward his owner, who was in the back yard, for some reason, hitting golf balls. Crazy bastard! When our friendly dog followed the black dog home, and he got near the crazy bastard, the crazy man swung whatever golf club he had at our dog's legs. It was awful to see. The dog went down and could barely walk back to our house. He collapsed on our lawn, and we had to carry him into the house."

Dr. Riley said, "What kind of dog was your dog, and what kind of dog is the neighbor's?"

"Ours is a Pit bull, but…but…he's very friendly. I should say he was very friendly. I don't know what kind of dog the crazy man's is, but he was very vicious. Barking, with bared teeth, the whole time."

"And how did you decide to put down your dog?"

"He was wildly whining and crying. It was obvious his legs were broken."

"Did you take the dog to the vets for an examination?"

"No. We did not. It was obvious the dog was in pain. We had to do it, although we didn't want to."

"How did you put the dog down?"

"One of the other men in the house did it. I don't know how."

Dr. Riley continued, "Do you have guns in the house?"

"We do not. We are peace-loving people, just like our dogs."

"Then what happened to the other dog, and what kind of dog was that?"

"He was a Doberman. When the maniac next door drove his little cart out to the middle of fairway, right there, the Doberman went out to say hello. Very friendly dog. But the maniac shined this very bright light in the dog's eyes. The dog didn't know where he was. When he was blinded, the crazy man hit him right on the head with the golf club. The dog went down and didn't move. The man drove off in his funny little cart, with the bright light shining ahead of him. We went out and had to pick up the poor dog and carry him back to our house."

"And one of your men put that dog out of his misery as well?"

"Yes. It was the humane thing to do."

Duarte said, "Can we see the other dogs? What breed are they?

"We have two more Dobermans and one more Pit. They are in the house, but you don't have to go in there. The dogs are fine."

Riley said, "We have to insist, actually. We can come back with a warrant, or you can just let us go in the house and see the remaining dogs."

"I'll go get them, then, and bring them out here."

Duarte and Riley were left alone in the back yard, and both felt there was more to this story. Something was strange about Whitebread. They walked to the end of the property and glanced over at Chipper's estate and his yard.

Whitebread came back carrying the Pit bull, and the Dobermans slinked along behind him, barely able to stand up. He said, "See how calm they are. Always like this. Very calm and peaceful." The dogs lay down on the lawn and could barely stay awake.

Riley put her hands on each dog and leaned over to rub each of them over most of their bodies. "These dogs appear to be drugged, Mr. Whitebread. Are they drugged?"

"No. Very calm and peaceful dogs. Always like this."

"I know a drugged dog when I see one, Mr. Whitebread."

"You are wrong. Always like this."

Duarte said, "Well, Mr. Whitebread. We'll go visit your neighbor and see what he has to say for himself."

Whitebread said, "Be careful if he is carrying a golf club. Very strange man."

As Riley and Duarte walked out of the yard, Riley commented, "Jacob, those dogs were very drugged. They should probably have their stomachs pumped. I have a hunch they are very wild and not peaceful and calm. We'll see. We should come back one day without telling this man. Also, from feeling and looking at their necks, it's obvious they had collars on, and they have an electrified virtual fence around the back yard. Their necks show abrasions from the collars and some burns from when they mistakenly went too far into the electrified field near the boundary."

They drove over to Chipper's, next door, but were unable to get in the estate gate. They wrote down the address, and later that day found Chipper Blair's contact information.

Bill Whitebread dragged the dogs back into the house and again locked them in a bedroom. He forgot to close the front gate to the estate.

IRENE MCVAY

Irene McVay was asked by both Chipper and Richard Stein to try to find anything about the Whitebread estate. She was apprised by Stein that it was probably not a coincidence that her tenant was calling himself Greg Whitebread, that the name of the man who purchased the estate next to Chipper was Todd Whitebread, and that the group renting Stein's new estate was also named Whitebread.

Irene dutifully agreed to visit the Whitebread estate, unannounced, and see what she could find out about the occupants. She went over the same day as the SPCA investigators and was surprised to find the front gate wide open. She was equally surprised that there were no cars in the driveway. She was on her way to the Pebble Beach Tennis Club and was dressed casually in her tennis outfit: blue tennis shorts and a pink tank top. She also had on a white visor with the Pebble Beach logo.

Irene had practiced her pitch several times and was prepared to say, "Hi, neighbor. I am Irene McVay of the Pebble Beach homeowners association. I want to welcome you to the neighborhood. I live down the road a little bit. May I come in and chat?"

No one answered the door when she knocked. She rang the bell, and no one answered. Bill Whitebread was in the house but didn't want to see anyone else that day. He wondered how someone had gotten through the front gate without ringing but quickly realized he forgot to close the gate after the inspectors left. He chastised himself. This was a horrible day.

Irene knocked again harder, and the front door opened a bit. She boldly opened it all the way and walked into the foyer. It was filled with cardboard boxes, all having Arabic language writing on them, metal containers with hazardous waste labels, some empty five-gallon water bottles, three hand trucks, and several prayer rugs. She wasn't afraid and tried to look in the cardboard boxes. She stayed away from the metal containers.

Bill Whitebread heard the front door open and silently walked toward the foyer. He was taken aback when he peeked around a wall and saw a strange woman in a tennis outfit snooping around the boxes. He panicked, grabbed one of the five-gallon bottles, and hit Irene on the back of the head as hard as he could. She went down on the floor without a whimper and lay still. She was out cold.

Whitebread still wasn't thinking clearly when he picked her up in a fireman's carry and deposited her on the floor in the kitchen/utility/ pantry room. He made sure to check her pockets, shorts, and top to see if she had a cell phone or car keys with her. She didn't. The utility room had no windows. Whitebread had mixed feelings when he saw she was still breathing and had no blood around her head. He left her in a heap on the floor and locked the room from the outside. He was positive she would not get out of her confinement until someone unlocked the door and got her out.

Irene woke up with a splitting headache and stayed on the cold floor in fetal position until her head stopped spinning. It was pitch dark, except for a small sliver of light around what looked like a door a few feet away from her. It took her a good five minutes to remember she was in the estate house next to Chipper's. The last thing she remembered was standing in the foyer looking at some strange boxes. Irene struggled to get to her knees and touched her head to see what hurt so much. She felt a large lump on the back of her head. She was still dizzy and decided to lay back down on the cold floor until the spinning stopped. It didn't.

She couldn't see but rose to her feet and held on to what felt like shelves to her left. She reached for the door and felt around for the door handle. It didn't turn. She tried to push on the door with no success. Irene felt her pockets to see if she had her cell phone and was disappointed she left it in her car. It never occurred to her that she might be in further danger from whoever conked her on the head. She screamed once, waited, then screamed louder. She stepped back a few steps and lunged at the door. It didn't open and now her shoulder hurt as well as her head. She started pounding on the door.

After ten minutes of screaming and pounding, she was exhausted and curled up again on the floor near the door. Maybe she would hear someone outside. Irene McVay fell asleep.

JENNY AND CHIPPER

Chipper woke up very early the next morning. He wanted to play more holes and loved that his light enabled him to play in the dark, because it created daylight conditions. He woke up Jenny by rubbing her shoulders gently. She was dazed and said, "Chipper. I want a baby. I think I want to have a baby."

He said, "Go back to sleep, Jenny. You are just dreaming. Go back to your dreams."

She sat up immediately and looked him right in the eyes. "Seriously, Chipper, I've been thinking about it since we got married. I think the best time is NOW!"

"You mean right this minute? I have to get up, so I can get to work on time. I think you've been listening to your mother's pep talks too much."

"I don't mean trying right now this morning but soon. I would love to have a baby Chipper or baby Jenny. I'm ready."

"I'm not sure I'm ready," Chipper said quietly.

"You think about it then today, Mr. Chips. I'm serious. Life is great. Think how great it would be to have a little one."

"Why don't we decide to have a baby when one of us makes the morning shot? Then we know it's fate, and the universe is ready for our baby."

"That's crazy. That leaves it up to blind luck. We might never make the morning shot! And you know what happened to Ben when he finally made it. He died immediately. That was it. That might happen to us."

"I have to get up. We're a lot younger than Ben, and our golf is much better, too. I might make the shot this morning."

"OK. We'll talk about it later. You try really hard to make it and run back in and tell me if you do. I'm going back to sleep. See you later. Have a good day at work. Be careful out there." Jenny kissed Chipper on the forehead, then rolled over and fell immediately to sleep.

When Chipper went outside in complete darkness and cold, he turned on his magic light and illuminated the entire area. He was happy to see no dogs or people in the neighbor's yard. He hoped Angus was doing OK at Irene's house. The poor dog had been through some trauma. Angus needed his morning runs. Chipper hit a great shot from his back yard to about six feet from the pin. It was not a baby-generating shot, however. Close, but no baby.

Chipper was able to play his way in, enjoying his route from Pebble to Spyglass to MPCC and then Spanish Bay. He noticed several more lights coming on at fairway estates as he created early morning daylight and brightness. He didn't think anything of it.

When Jenny drove her electric Jaguar out the front gate of their estate, she was surprised her way was blocked by several, she counted seven, people carrying signs. When they saw the gate open, they started marching in circles, chanting and impeding her way out.

"*Dog Killer! Dog Killer! Dog Killer!*"

"*You are the beast!*"

"*You are inhumane!*"

"*You are scum!*"

"*Dog Killer! Dog Killer! Dog Killer!*"

Jenny had no idea what they were doing there or what they were talking about. She opened her window hesitantly and asked politely what they were up to. One of the protestors came up to the window and said, "Are you Mrs. Blair? Your husband is a dog killer. He killed the dogs next door. How can you be married to such a man? Such a beast. Animal abuser."

"I have no idea what you are talking about. My husband is a kind man. There were some dogs attacking our dog, and he protected our poor Angus. That's all he did."

"Not according to the news yesterday."

"I was not aware of any news about this. It was nothing but protecting our dog."

"You should read the online article, then."

"I will. Can I go to work now, please? My husband is not in the house. He leaves very early in the morning. Protesting and marching here won't help you in any way."

"We want to send a message to your neighbors all around here. Go ahead and leave, but we'll be here today and probably for several days. Your husband has to come out one of these times."

"Don't count on it," Jenny said, as she closed her car window.

She looked at the signs they held.

ANIMAL KILLER LIVES HERE

BEWARE THE BEAST IN THIS HOUSE

DOG LOVERS UNITE

CHIPPER BLAIR IS A DOG KILLER

PETA ISSUES A WARNING ABOUT THIS HOUSE

PEBBLE BEACH COMPANY
MORNING MEETING

Richard Stein walked into the conference room twenty seconds before the meeting was scheduled to start. Everyone of importance was already seated. As he came in the door, he said loudly, "We have some real issues about the visiting Arabs, who claim they are from LIV. They also claim to all have the last name Whitebread. I think that is a joke with them. Let me…"

Stevens held up his arm and waved for Stein to stop. He waved frantically for a few seconds, then said, "It can't be as important, Richard, as that asshole Blair causing trouble again. It really can't…"

"Oh, but it is Donald. I think they are plotting something…"

"Don't interrupt me, Stein. Really. Don't interrupt me. Did you see that Blair killed a couple of dogs living next door to him? What the hell is the guy thinking? He used his golf clubs again. Killed some friendly dogs, according to the Herald article. He just can't keep out of trouble. Every time this happens, it looks bad for the Corporation. Real bad. The public sometimes forgives people killers, but never do they forgive animal abusers. Never!"

Stein stammered, "I'm sure he had a good reason. Have you heard his side of the story?"

"You're always protecting him, Stein. Why is that? Are you a horrible judge of character? The guy is nothing but a maniac. Nothing but trouble. This is the last straw. I want him fired, Roger! Fire him today!"

Roger Hennessey commented, "But Donald. Shouldn't we hear his side of the story?"

"NO! I never want to hear his name again. Please. Never again!" Stevens stood up and started walking around the table nervously. "Is everything OK for the golf tournament? Any issues?"

Stein, who was still standing as well, said, "Donald. I think Chipper Blair...

Stevens yelled, "I told you I never wanted to hear his name again! Never again!"

Stein continued, "is the least of your problems. I think the Arabs are planning something really bad. I don't know what but really bad. Just a hunch. My friend Irene McVay, who lives off the eleventh fairway, rented her guest house to another guy named Whitebread. She found some plans for the ballrooms at both the Lodge and Spanish Bay in one of the drawers near his bed. What would he need those for? And the Whitebreads who rented my house changed the locks, so I can't get in the gate. The Whitebreads who paid an exorbitant price for the estate next to..." Stein hesitated because he didn't want to say Chipper again... "off the fourteenth fairway, seem very suspicious as well."

Stevens replied, "Just because they are all Arabs doesn't make them someone to fear. The guy in the guest house may just be studying ballroom plans for future LIV functions, both here and at their events. The only thing we use the ballroom for during tournament week is the Clambake event. We don't even use the Spanish Bay ballroom. It's irrelevant to me. Just calm down, Richard. I know you are Jewish. You probably have a fear or bias against Arabs anyway."

"I called the D.A.'s office and the sheriff's office, and they won't go investigate, and they won't help me get in my own property. I asked Irene

McVay to go over to the Whitebreads off of fourteen and see if she could just be a friendly neighbor and get a look inside the house. Why would they pay seventy-five million cash for a house only worth less than half of that?"

CO McDougall commented, "Calm down, Richard. When you have billions, what's another thirty or forty million?" This drew laughs from everyone around the table.

Stein continued, "I haven't heard from Irene McVay yet. I hope to hear from her soon."

"Get your act together, Stein. Concentrate on what you are supposed to be doing here. Legal stuff and community relations. Don't stir up trouble. And my next issue is we had about a dozen angry callers leaving messages this morning about the strange bright light on the fairways just before dawn. Do we have UFOs? Both from Pebble and Spyglass. They claim it's us, and we're doing stuff before the ATT. We're not! I'm going to send a few security guides out really early tomorrow to both the fourteenth and fifteenth holes at Pebble and the back nine at Spyglass and see if they can figure out what is going on. What a morning: Arab spies, UFOs, more trouble for Blair, killed some dogs, crazy, crazy, crazy! It's not like I don't have enough to worry about."

On the way out, Roger Hennessey said to Stein, "Donald never goes over to Spanish Bay, does he? I have no intention of firing Chipper. Donald will never see him over there. There must be a good story behind this animal abuse thing."

Stein commented, "Donald never goes over there. Correct. Chipper probably killed the dogs, though. I can see him doing that."

SPANISH BAY FIRST TEE

Chipper had a wonderful morning at the first tee at Spanish Bay. It wasn't too crowded, and he was able to hit about a dozen drives down the first fairway, making several groups teeing off very happy when he told them to pick up and keep the Titleist Pro-V1s they find. The fairway was wide enough that he never missed it. The balls were easy to find. He amused a few groups when they asked him where the best place to hit their drives was and he shined the tactical flashlight beam on laser mode right down the middle.

Just before noon, though, things started getting exciting. The sun finally came out. Chipper watched as Patrick Cantlay and Xander Schauffele came slowly down the clubhouse stairs toward the first tee. Their caddies, Joe LaCava and Austin Kaiser, followed behind. Kaiser and LaCava were almost as recognizable as their pro counterparts because of all their TV time. Some tourists stared at the group as they walked to the tee.

Chipper had played some junior golf with both of them a long time ago and was sure they would not recognize him. He wasn't a big fan of Cantlay. Didn't like his personality, his slow play, and many of his recent comments about pro golf and golfers. He liked to call him "Can't Play."

Cantlay walked right up to Chipper and said, "You look familiar to me." He looked at his name tag and then said, "I know you. We played in a North vs. South Junior match a long time ago."

Chipper said, "Yes. I beat you on the last hole. I was fifteen, and you were seventeen. You should remember that."

"I don't quite remember it that way," Cantlay said. Schauffele came wandering over as well.

"I remember you too, Blair. How's it going? We're up here for practice rounds week after next at Pebble and Spy and wanted to play here before it's renovated. Neither of us have ever played it before. Then we can compare before and after. I hear it's kind of a dog track now but Gil is going to make it first rate."

Chipper winced at Schauffele calling Spyglass "Spy." Would it be so hard to say the entire name?

Cantlay said, "I see you never made it to the tour. Did you ever try?"

"I don't hit it far enough. Knew I wouldn't make it," was all Chipper said. Then he added, "I don't see you guys on the starter sheet. Did you have a time? Can I see your receipt?"

Cantlay looked at him with a strange look and took a step back before saying, "The guys in the clubhouse said there was an opening and just head to the first tee. I don't see anyone waiting to tee off."

"I'm not supposed to let anyone tee off without a receipt. Go up there and get a receipt. Then I can let you play."

Both Cantlay and Schauffele looked at each other before Xander asked his caddie Austin to trudge up the stairs and get a receipt. Neither was very happy and let Chipper know it with their glares. The group stood in silence and watched the caddy head up into the clubhouse and then return waiving a piece of paper. Chipper took the receipt and then watched them tee off.

As they were about to leave the tee, Chipper said, "Do me a favor. Let me hit a drive and you, maybe Joe, can signal back in some way how many yards I was behind you? Wave his arm once for every ten yards. That would be great. Thank you, Joe. How is Tiger, by the way?"

Chipper hit quickly and watched as his ball flew right down the middle. No one said anything. Chipper watched as LaCava reached Chipper's ball, put it in Cantlay's golf bag, and waved back to the tee. His left arm waved once, twice, three, four, five times. Chipper said out loud, "Fifty yards. Probably two eighty to three thirty. I hit that one pretty well. That's why Chipper Blair is not on the tour."

About ten minutes later, his phone rang. It was Emily Hastings. She said, "Hi Chipper, have you seen Irene in the last few days? She was supposed to meet me and Tak for a morning run/walk. She never misses a day, but she hasn't been here. I called her cell, and she didn't answer. I texted also, but I didn't get any reply. I'm a little worried."

"I haven't heard from her. She has Angus in her house. I'm sure everything is fine. Maybe she just slept in. Did you call Big Bill?"

"I did call Bill. He said he was going over there early evening today after work and would call me then."

"I'm sure everything is OK, Emily. Don't worry. You'll never guess who just teed off over here at Spanish Bay? Patrick Can't Play and Xander Schauffele."

Emily said, "Who? I don't know who they are. Funny names."

"Number four and five ranked golfers in the world, Emily. You should know their names."

"I don't care, Chipper. Can't Play is a funny name for a golfer, isn't it?"

"Yes it is, Emily. Have a good day. If I hear anything from Irene, I'll call you."

The tee was empty, and Chipper closed his eyes and stared toward the sun for a minute to soak in the heat. He still had warming gloves on his hands. When he opened his eyes, a few men in matching clothes were coming down the stairs. They had on black slacks and light colored golf shirts but no golf clubs. When they wandered over to Chipper on the first tee, he could see the shirt logo said SPCA.

The bigger man came up to Chipper and didn't put out his hand to shake. He just said, "Mr. Blair. We were told we would find you here. My name is Jacob Dunne. I am the SPCA investigations supervisor. This is my boss Mr. Scott Delucchi. He is the CEO of the Monterey County SPCA. We wanted to come out and talk to you. There have been some serious allegations against you for animal abuse…"

Chipper interrupted, "This all so much blown out of proportion. I was just protecting our little dog, Angus. He's a Scottie. Very smart dog."

"Not according to the Whitebreads, who live next door to you…"

Chipper interrupted again, "They are scarily crazy, and their dogs are violent. I haven't met them yet."

Delucchi said, "Mr. Blair. Please don't interrupt. Just let Mr. Dunne ask you questions, and you answer. I don't think you understand how serious this matter is. They allege you killed their dogs. It's a felony, you know. You could have a huge fine and go to jail for this. Please just answer Mr. Dunne's questions. We are recording you, as well."

"If someone comes to the tee to play, then I have to help them. That's my job. Go ahead and fire away with the questions. Do I need a lawyer?"

Delucchi said, "I don't know. Do you?"

"Just ask your questions," Chipper said. He grabbed his driver, because he felt more comfortable holding the golf club when he was answering questions. When he grabbed his driver, both Delucchi and Dunne stepped back several steps. Chipper just smiled and didn't say anything.

Dunne started, "Just tell me your side of the story, Mr. Blair. Make it as short or as long as you want. Just so we understand what happened from your viewpoint."

Chipper showed pictures of Angus on his phone to the SPCA guys adding, "This is our vicious little black dog."

Scott Delucchi said, "Isn't he the dog that was dragging the woman into the falling tree at Spyglass Hill late last year? She got crushed by the tree, right? Dog walked away with no injuries? That little black dog? We keep track of all these things, you know. No one ever filed charges."

"He helped save the Del Monte Forest. This little dog did this."

"Still, she got crushed, right?"

"She deserved it. Evil woman."

"And you decide who deserves death and who is evil?"

"She was evil. No doubt about it."

Jacob Duarte said, "You are off to a very bad start, Mr. Blair. Really bad start!"

Chipper then told his story. "I'll give you the short version. The strange men moved into the house next door to us when we were on our honeymoon. We have never met them and still have not met them. We, me and my wife Jenny, get up very early, and take one golf shot each from our back yard, to the fourteenth green. Angus likes to chase the balls and brings them back. The first morning back, we saw five dogs in the back yard of the Whitebreads. That's what they call themselves. Three Dobermans and two Pit bulls. When we hit our shots and Angus went by their property the five wild dogs started rampaging toward Angus. They were apparently wearing collars, because when they reached the end of their property, they were stunned by an invisible electric fence. One Pit bull made it through, very shocked, and headed toward Angus. Angus was petrified and was heading back toward me. Just before the Pit reached Angus, I hit him in the legs with the golf club I was holding. It took the legs out from under him, and he turned around and headed back home. He was able to get back to the property of the Whitebreads on his own. My wife took poor Angus in the house. I take my golf cart into work on the golf course, always. I drove out to the fourteenth fairway and I guess the Whitebreads turned off their electric fence, because one of the Dobermans came out on the fairway charging at me with teeth showing. He was trying to kill me and jump in the cart."

At this point Chipper showed the men his flashlight and shined it down the fairway. "I shined this thing in his eyes, and he couldn't see. When he leaped at me, I hit him on the head with my golf club. He went down, and I drove away. Don't know what happened to the dog. Either dog." Chipper was done and waited for a comment from either man.

Delucchi finally said, "When we visited the neighbor, Bill Whitebread said they had to put both dogs down, because they were maimed so badly by you." Chipper just looked at the men and didn't say anything. All three just stared at each other without speaking.

Duarte finally said, "Two pretty different stories, but honestly, Mr. Blair, there never is a reason to hit a dog with a golf club. Never."

"What would you do if a Doberman and a Pit bull were charging you or your dog and you had a golf club in your hand? Just say, nice doggie, please stop?"

"Thank you, Mr. Blair. Thanks for your time. We'll go back and see the remaining dogs and ask Bill Whitebread more questions. We might have to charge you with felonious animal abuse. Don't leave town."

THE WHITEBREAD PANTRY

Irene McVay was shivering on the floor of the Whitebread's utility room. It was dark. She wished she would have worn her sweats rather than just her tennis shorts and shirt. She was hungry, tired, and afraid. She rose to her knees and her head was still throbbing. She used the shelves to help her stand up and started to feel around to see if there was any food. The kept touching bottles on a few shelves but then on the third shelf she felt some plastic packages that gave her some optimism. She grabbed a few of them and returned to the cold floor and crawled over near the door where there was a small amount of light at the bottom.

When she saw one package was Pita Bread, she opened it quickly and grabbed two of them at the same time. She rolled up two of them and started chewing them violently. She thought to herself that at least she wouldn't starve in here.

When she had eaten four of them, she again lie on the floor and tried to decide if it was day or night. Irene wasn't sure how much time had gone by but she finally heard several voices outside her door. She stood slowly and started yelling and pounding on the door. "Let me out! Whoever you are? Let me out of here!" She screamed and pounded until she was exhausted and then slumped to the floor with her back leaning on the door. She heard the door handle start to turn and when it opened she fell backward to the floor. Someone was grabbing her by the arms and dragging her backward on the floor. It hurt her back. She heard several voices talking in what sounded like Arabic.

Her eyes took some adjusting. She could see the ceiling and that she was back in the foyer. Several men, she counted six, were standing over her shouting at each other in Arabic. No question this time they were Arabs. Two were wearing kaffiyehs. The man who looked the oldest was doing most of the yelling. When her eyes focused, she recognized her tenant Greg Whitebread, as one of the men standing over her. Greg Whitebread was talking animatedly in Arabic.

The older man in the kaffiyeh looked down at her and in perfect English said, "What are you doing in our house? Why are you here?"

Although she was having trouble concentrating Irene said what she had been practicing, "I live nearby and I was sent by the homeowners group to welcome you to the neighborhood. We like to do that for all the new people." She then looked at her tenant and said, "Hello Greg. What are you doing here?"

Greg Whitebread said, "The question is, Irene, what are you doing here? You aren't really a close neighbor. Your house is more than a mile away. We are not neighbors at all."

"Everyone in Pebble Beach is a neighbor. It's a very small area actually. We greet all the new neighbors. We're very friendly here. Can I stand up, please? I think I need to stand up. My head hurts and the floor is very cold. What is it? Marble?"

No one helped her up and she staggered to her feet and leaned against the wall. She was now very afraid. The older man said, "Why did you come in the house? Is it neighborly to enter someone's house when no one is here?"

He looked at the other men and started yelling at one of them in Arabic. He called him Jamal. Jamal bolted toward the front door but the other four men grabbed him and restrained him by the arms very quickly.

The older man then said in English, "Jamal. You are an idiot. You have brought attention to our house. You have done very badly. You should have let the dogs just go and not called anyone. You have hit this woman. Now what do we do with this woman? We cannot let her go. What do you suppose we do with her? Just what should we do Jamal? You are an idiot."

He then took out a gun from his pant waistband and pointed it at Irene's head. She closed her eyes and slumped to the floor. As she slid down the wall to the floor she heard a loud bang from the gun. On the floor, she was surprised she wasn't hit. She opened her eyes in time to see Jamal, with a bullet hole in his head, bleeding profusely on the marble, and the other four men around him. They all had shocked looks on their faces and started yelling wildly. They were yelling at Ali, who was evidently their leader and the man with the gun.

Ali held up his hand to quiet everyone and they immediately obeyed. He said calmly, "Do the Khashoggi thing on him. Do it in here so the marble will be easy to clean up. Get rid of him. Stupid Jamal." He pointed at the man Irene knew as Greg and said, "Hassan. Drive her car back to her house, clean your prints, leave her phone and whatever else is in there, and just leave it in her driveway. Be careful. "Before you go put her back in the closet and leave her there. Make sure she can't get out. Not sure what we'll do with her. Probably same thing as Jamal. I need time to think."

Irene didn't struggle when Hassan helped her get up and put her back in the utility room. She said, "Hassan, huh? What are you guys up to?" He shoved her into the closet, locked the door, and didn't reply. Irene sat down and started sobbing.

BIG BILL O'SHEA

Irene McVay's current beau, Big Bill O'Shea, clicked the gate key of Irene's estate. The gate slid back and he drove into the driveway. He was there for his every other night dinner and sleepover. He had called Irene earlier in the day, and she didn't answer. Her car was in the driveway, up near the front door. He figured she was home and was eager to see what she was cooking for dinner. He was even more eager for the after-dinner activities. Irene was still an exciting and vibrant woman at almost sixty years old.

He looked in her car, and Irene's cell phone was on the driver's seat, as well as her purse. He figured she must have just driven home, rushed in the house, and was planning on coming back for her stuff. He had a key to the front door, but he rang the bell anyway before just opening the lock. In the entrance hall, he yelled, "Irene! Hey sweetie, where are you?" She had played games like this before with him. He ran upstairs to the bedroom and hoped she was in the bed naked. No such luck today. He continued calling her name but with no response.

Bill looked all over the house, in the wine cellar, in the kitchen, then headed to the back yard and guest house to see if the tenant had seen or heard from her. He had never met the tenant, wasn't happy she had a tenant, and looked forward with some anticipation, of meeting the man. He knocked on the door, and Greg Whitebread opened it a crack and peered out at Big Bill O'Shea. O'Shea was an impressive looking man with short gray hair, tall, with a husky build.

Without waiting for a word from Whitebread, O'Shea said, "Hello. I'm Irene's friend Bill, have you seen her today?" O'Shea was surprised to see the good looking Arab man's face in the doorway.

Whitebread said, "I have not seen her today. I don't see her much at all."

"Thank you. I'll be in the house tonight. It's very strange that her car is here, but she is not."

"Maybe she took a walk or something?"

"That would be highly unlikely. I've never known her to do that, and she was expecting me tonight for dinner."

Whitebread said quickly, "Sorry I could not help you," and shut the door.

Big Bill walked back to the main house and when inside called his friend, Chipper. "Chipper. Irene is not here. I'm getting very worried. She's never done this before. Her car is in the driveway with her phone and purse. I'm going to get those and put them in the house. She is not around, though."

Chipper said, "Stein told me he was expecting her to call but hadn't heard from her either. He told me he had sent her over to my neighbor's to see if she could find out something about them. He wanted her to call him back with what she saw."

"I don't imagine she walked over there. It's quite a way. No one has heard from her, then, for two days. That's crazy. I'm going to go over to your neighbors and see what they have to say. If I can't find anything about her and I don't hear from her tonight, I'm going to report her missing and get the sheriff's department or Pebble Beach security involved. Stein can do that for me, right?"

"Yes, please," said Chipper. "I'm getting worried, too. Something strange is going on in that house right now. Do you know they reported me for animal abuse?"

"Yes. Everyone knows that, Chipper. It seems like every few months you get accused of something."

"You know I just try to play golf and stay out of trouble, Bill. None of this is ever my fault."

O'Shea just laughed and said, "Yeah. Yeah. It's never your fault, Chipper."

Chipper commented, "I'll be home pretty soon. Is Angus at Irene's? He's supposed to be there. I hope he's there. Can you see if you can find him and bring him back over here? If Irene isn't there, the little guy must be very hungry. Maybe just let Angus off near our driveway. He knows how to get in between the rungs of the gate. Then, after you go to the neighbors, come by and have a drink and talk. We can call Stein then and see what he has to say. Be careful over there."

O'Shea started yelling for Angus on the first floor of the house with no luck. Then he went back up to the bedroom and yelled again, and Angus came out from under the bed and rubbed against Big Bill's leg. Bill picked him up with one large hand under the belly and hugged Angus. Angus licked his face. There was no indication Angus was hungry. Bill went outside, put Angus in the driver's side seat and then drove over to Chipper's and dropped him off. Then he went next door to the Whitebread's estate.

He hit the intercom button outside the gate. No one answered, so he hit the button several times again. No one replied. He then drove next door to Chipper's and just waited outside the gate. It was dark. While Bill waited, he called Stein and told Stein to come over to Chipper's for a discussion of what to do about Irene McVay. Stein said he felt guilty, because both Chipper and he had asked Irene to check on the Whitebreads.

Jenny drove up and opened the gate and watched as Big Bill came driving in behind her. She greeted him warmly when they both had parked. "I'm worried about Irene, Jenny, she's not been seen for a few days. Didn't come home. Her car is in her driveway, and her phone and purse are in the front seat. She would never go anywhere without those. Never!"

"Don't worry, Bill. She is very resourceful and tough. I'm sorry to say this, but you know her, maybe she met someone and is just hidden away for a few days. It wasn't that long ago she went away with Bradenton, the head of the board at Cypress."

Bill grimaced, "Thanks, Jenny. Bad memory. I'm sure she wouldn't do that, and if she did, she would have called me. She trusts me. She didn't take her phone. I am really worried."

They went in the house, and Angus was in the foyer. He intelligently had gone around the house and entered through the Baboni 3-Flaps Pet Door they had installed recently. It had a steel frame and telescoping tunnel. Angus barked at Jenny and waited to be picked up. She obliged. "Glad to see you back home, Angus. Really glad to see you," she said.

Jenny and Bill headed to the pub and waited for Chipper and Richard Stein. Jenny opened a beer for Bill and made herself a martini. Stein knew to just enter the house and head downstairs. Chipper came down about the same time. Angus was in his glory when all of his friends were seated and drinking. He was alternately rubbing each person's legs under the table.

Jenny started, "Before we get to Irene, I want to call the SPCA animal control and have them come over here early in the morning. They can watch our shots and learn to know Angus and hopefully the dogs next door will be in the neighbor's yard and the electric gate will be on. It's time we ended this accusation stuff. Jerry Devine shouldn't have printed anything in the paper about this. I thought he was our friend."

Chipper just commented, "Must have been a slow news day." He sipped on his scotch.

Jenny called the SPCA and left a message. She hoped they would listen to the message and come over early in the morning. She told them she would leave their front gate open and they should just come around to the back yard at six thirty.

Chipper wasn't happy. He knew he couldn't get in his morning golf holes. He was going to have to drive to work.

Bill said, "I understand you guys asked Irene to check out the neighbor's house? Not sure that was a good idea. Why didn't you just send Pebble Beach security in there, Richard?"

Stein said, "There wasn't sufficient reason to do that. Now, I think that there is. I can have them go tomorrow morning. I'll call the Monterey County Sheriff's Department, too. Did I tell you Irene found diagrams of the ballrooms at the Lodge and Spanish Bay in her tenant's place? Very suspicious. They are supposed to be here to watch the ATT and get ideas for LIV tournaments. I don't know why they would need the ballroom diagrams, especially Spanish Bay. Nothing is going on at Spanish Bay during tournament week."

Big Bill was on his second beer and announced, "I'm just going to go over there now and find out what's up. I'll go in through the back yard."

Chipper said, "How much of an electric charge can you take, Bill? They have the electrified fence that I am sure is on now. Then the remaining killer dogs would get you after that. Two Dobermans and a Pit bull."

"I'm going anyway," Bill declared loudly and started to get up.

Jenny pushed him down in the chair and said, "No you don't, Bill. I'll make you a martini. Just sit still, and we'll let the sheriff deal with this tomorrow."

IRENE ON THE MOVE

Irene spent a sleepless night in the utility room. She was sobbing, hungry, and cold. Every thirty minutes she would pound on the door and yell; sometimes just screaming and sometimes yelling "Let me out!" All she ate was pita bread that she found in abundance on one of the shelves. She couldn't help thinking to herself that she would never get out of the closet. *This was it. I'm going to die in this closet. And I look awful. My hair is a mess. My clothes are dirty. I hope no one sees me like this. These white tennis clothes are dirty. A mess. My hair must look awful.* Then Irene McVay started praying and talking to her dead husband. She lay on the cold floor and mumbled for what seemed like hours.

At some point she heard voices outside her chamber. They were speaking in Arabic. She stood up and pounded on the door and yelled at the top of her lungs with what felt like the only energy she had. "Let me out! Let me out! Let me out!" She heard the door handle being unlocked, and the door started to open. It was dark, and she couldn't see. She leaned on the door and fell on the floor toward the voices. She was quickly kicked in the ribs and let out a scream of pain.

One of the men yelled in English, "Shut up! Just shut up, or I will kick you again!"

Irene, in pain, yelled back, "Fuck you! Let me out! Let me go!" The man kicked her in the ribs again, only harder. She writhed in pain on the ground. I was still dark, and her eyes didn't adjust.

She couldn't see, and her side was wracked with severe pain. The men started jabbering in Arabic again, then one of the voices said, "Hassan, why don't you just shoot her now, and we'll Khashoggi her. Right here and now! What do we want with her?"

Hassan said slowly and deliberately, "We might need her later. People may be looking for her now. We have to take her to the other house. Get her out of here and put her in a locked room in the rental house. We'll deal with her later. Just get her out of this house."

One of the men put a trash bag over Irene's head and picked her up on his shoulder. She kicked her legs violently, even though it hurt her side. She felt another man grab her legs, and she relaxed a bit. She couldn't move. The men started talking in Arabic again. The only English word she heard uttered a few times was "Clambake." She thought to herself, *What the hell does that mean? Where are they taking me?*

Irene almost passed out from her pain and her hunger. She was thrown in the back seat of one of the black Escalades. One man sat on her back and another on her legs. She kept saying, "You are hurting me. Get off me. Where are you taking me?" After a short drive, she was dragged out of the back seat and carried again. She was deposited in another cold room on the floor, kicked again in the side. The trash bag was still over her head. When she heard the door slam and lock, she slipped off the trash bag, struggled to her feet and found a light switch.

She smiled as she realized she was in Emily Hasting's wine cellar, now Richard Stein's wine cellar. She had been in this room many times. She thought to herself, *Can I live on wine and liquor alone? I hope some of the wine has screw tops. I'm sure I can open some of the expensive champagne.* Then she winced in pain, slumped to the floor and started screaming again.

ANIMAL ABUSE

The next morning Chipper was anxious to get in his cart and play some holes on the way to Spanish Bay. He didn't think the animal abuse officers would hear Jenny's message in time to be at his house this early in the morning. Jenny and Chipper paced back and forth in their entrance hall, with the front door open, and waited. Angus paced back and forth with them.

A few times Jenny knelt and put her hands on Angus's face, stared him in the eyes, and made sure he was paying attention. "Angus. I want you to be on your best behavior. Be calm. Be nice. Be your best self. If these men have uniforms on, don't let that scare you. Show them your personality. You are the best, Angus!"

Chipper said, "Do you really think he knows what you are saying? Really, Jenny."

She gave Chipper a hug and replied, "You know he does, Mr. Chips. He absolutely does. Don't you, Angus?" Angus tilted his head and looked at her quizzically. Then he barked three times.

After several minutes, they saw the SPCA van pull in near the front door and park. They were surprised to see two men and one woman get out of the van. It was CEO Scott Delucchi, Investigator Jacob Duarte, and the Senior Vet. Dr. Kate Riley. Each had a Starbucks cup of coffee in their hands. Delucchi immediately said, "It's good I listen to my messages at night. It's awfully early to make a house call." They were all in street clothes. No uniforms.

When they entered the house, Angus immediately walked up to Delucchi, rubbed against his leg, and lay on the floor on his back, waiting for a belly rub. Jenny said, "This is the vicious dog, Angus." Delucchi petted Angus vigorously.

Jenny commented again, "We wanted you here early to see exactly what we do in the morning and to meet Angus. We're hoping the dogs next door are in the yard this morning. Then you can meet them too."

Chipper said, "Do any of you play golf?"

Delucchi and Riley said, "Yes." Duarte said, "No."

As they walked through the house to the back door Delucchi commented, "Nice house. What do you guys do? If I may ask."

Chipper said, "We both are assistant golf pros at Pebble Beach."

"Pro golf must pay more than I think, then," Delucchi commented.

"We inherited the house. The man who gave us his house was Ben Morris, a wealthy Scotsman. Ben used to go outside in the morning and do this golf shot every morning. We do it now to honor Ben. He loved watching the ball in flight. He lived for that. So do I, actually."

Chipper grabbed four Slazengers from the bowl near the back door, and all of them except Angus walked out and started toward the steps to the back lawn. Angus hesitated. Jenny said, "Poor Angus is terrified to go outside now, because of the incident with the dogs next door." She picked up Angus and the SPCA people could see Angus was shaking a bit in her arms. She carried Angus down to the back yard. Angus stood between her legs when they all heard barking from next door.

Delucchi said, "Well, it seems the dogs are out. That's a good thing."

Chipper said, "I'm not so sure it's a good thing. We'll see. I hope they have their electric fence on."

The Vet said, "I examined the dogs next door and noticed they had signs of protective collars that were too tight around their necks. I figured there was an electric shock barrier around the back yard." The dogs, on cue, started barking loudly.

Chipper hit first and said, "That's a good one, probably ten feet left of the pin and about pin high."

Kate Riley commented, "How can you tell? It's pretty dark. I can barely follow the ball."

"I've done the shot enough times to know where it's going, based on the feel and how solidly I hit it."

"What kind of crazy club is that?"

"It's very old. It's called a long spoon. Ben used it. Very old club. Hard to hit. Ben used it, he claims, to make a birdie on the Road Hole at St. Andrews. I believe him. He was a good stick when he was younger. You try it next."

Riley took the club and started a few practice swings. Chipper said, "It's hard to hit. You have to wait for the club head a bit. Swing slower than you would with a regular club."

Jenny watched her swing and said, "Your grip is a little strong. Try moving your right hand more on top of your left. Move the V, the space between your thumb and forefinger, more to where it is pointing at the right side of your neck, instead of way off to the right."

Riley took a swing at the Slazenger and topped it a few feet in front of her only. "Let me hit another one."

Chipper said, "Ben's rule is only one per morning. Sorry. You'll have to come back some time."

"This Ben was quite a character, I see. I still want to hit another one, please."

"Maybe next time," Chipper said. "Rules are rules. Especially Ben's. If Angus wasn't so afraid of the dogs next door, he would have headed off toward the green to fetch my ball. He would bring it back and we'd give him seven treats. Now he's so afraid, he won't leave Jenny's legs to even fetch your ball. Only a few yards. It's very sad."

Jenny stepped up and hit a good one. "That one is probably about the same distance away as Chipper's. Maybe ten feet to the right of the pin. Let's walk Angus over toward the neighbors and see what happens. She picked up Angus and the five of them headed toward the Whitebread estate very slowly. They could hear the dogs snarling loudly and barking wildly as they approached. Both Delucchi and Duarte took what looked like taser guns out from their belts.

They saw the two Dobermans and the Pit bull running frantically right toward them. They pointed their tasers in the dog's direction. Angus was whining. As the dogs encountered the electric barrier, they all tumbled on the ground and whimpered in pain. They limped back toward the house. Jenny put Angus down on the ground, and the emboldened dog barked at the other dogs then took off toward the fourteenth green to fetch the golf balls.

They could hear a man's voice yelling from the back yard in Arabic. He was walking toward them yelling loudly. Then he switched to English and said, "Fuck you. What are you doing here harassing the dogs again? Get the Fuck away." Then he saw there were five people.

Delucchi said, "Sorry for this. Three of us are from the SPCA. Just checking out your complaint from a few days ago. Is Mr. Bill Whitebread here? He is the one who filed the complaint. Can I speak to Mr. Whitebread?"

The man said in broken English, "I am Whitebread. I am John Whitebread. Can I help?" He was almost laughing when he said he was Whitebread.

"We talked to Bill Whitebread last time we were here. He filed the complaint," Delucchi said.

"Bill is not living here anymore. He gone. He left. We don't want to file complaint anymore. No complaint. Dogs fine."

"I'm not sure we can disregard the complaint," Delucchi continued. Chipper and Jenny looked at each other with some alarm. "As we understand there are two dogs who were abused and are now dead. Is that right?"

"We don't want complaint. Forget it."

"How did the dogs die, then? Humanely?" said Dr. Riley.

"No difference. Dead now. What difference it make?"

"How did you kill them?"

"Don't know. Drop complaint," said Whitebread, and he started walking away.

Delucchi yelled after him. "We're not done yet Mr. Whitebread! We're not done!"

Angus came running back with the second golf ball and put it down at Delucchi's feet. The two Dobermans and the Pit bull were only several feet away but on the other side of the electric barrier. Angus seemed to wink at them before taking off running back to Chipper's back yard.

Chipper picked up the Slazenger and said, "So, I guess this is over?"

Delucchi said, "Not really. You clubbed the dogs, and they are dead in some way. We still have to follow up on this. There is a court complaint against you, as well as our abuse case. I can see your dog is docile, and these dogs are potentially violent, but that doesn't excuse you from clubbing the dogs. Why don't you get a taser for future possible incidents?"

Jenny was angry and said sarcastically, "Who carries a taser? Why would we carry a taser? This should never have happened. Chipper was just protecting Angus. Poor dog. You can see how frightened Angus was to come over here."

RICHARD STEIN

Stein arrived at work early and did his usual diligence in contacting everyone that he thought could help find Irene McVay. He was sure her disappearance was part of a larger plot by the Whitebreads to sabotage the upcoming golf tournament. There were too many strange things going on. Irene had been missing three or four days now. Stein called Officers Anderson and Henderson, of the Monterey County Sheriff's Office. He contacted the San Francisco FBI office and spoke to the Special Agent in charge, Robert Tripp. He tried to have his own Pebble Beach Corporation head of Security, Patrick Black, make a promise to investigate immediately.

Black was reluctant because he had enough on his plate already with the tournament coming up in less than a week. He told Stein that Stein was paranoid and not to worry about it. Tripp, in San Francisco, told Stein he would have two agents drive down, Elvis Chan and Agustin Lopez. Anderson and Henderson were skeptical but helped Stein fill out a missing person report that same early morning. Stein told them that the FBI agents from San Francisco were arriving the next day. Anderson wasn't happy with the thought of working with overbearing FBI agents. They would want to take over. Henderson also thought Stein was paranoid.

Stein walked into the morning meeting a bit late. Stevens was explaining that he had sent out three security guards in golf carts very early to investigate the strange lights that people off the fairways at Pebble and Spyglass had been complaining about. They found nothing. No lights. No persons of interest. The courses were empty, except for a few deer. And then he joked, "And the deer were not carrying big lights." No one laughed. Stevens said, "I'll send them out in the morning, as well, and see what happens. These people must all be hallucinating."

Stein thought this was a great opportunity to talk about security at the golf tournament and his suspicions about the Whitebreads. Patrick Black was seated next to him. He told the group his theory and about Irene McVay being missing, after he asked her to check out the Whitebread house on the fourteenth fairway. Stein also brought the group up to speed on his early morning phone calls to Anderson and Henderson, and the FBI office in San Francisco.

Stevens wasn't happy. "We don't need this now, Stein. I am sure Patrick has our security all under control." He looked at Patrick Black.

Black started, "We've been planning this since last year's tournament. We always hire three hundred extra security guards, many in plain clothes. This year we have close to four hundred. We have metal detectors at all entrances where there will be events or spectators coming in, including all entrance gates, all entrances to the Lodge, and at the Clambake entrance in the Lodge ballroom. We have done security checks of all volunteers, even volunteers we have used for years and years. We have drones planned this year. All the tickets have barcodes that we scan, so we know who is on course and who is coming in. We have covered everything. We'll go out and investigate Irene McVay's house and the Whitebread house today, as well. I'll go myself with two of our best security people. I am very confident. I can't imagine anything happening out of our control or visibility."

Stevens said, "Thank you, Patrick. I know you are the best. Richard, just calm down."

Stein said, "I just will feel better after all this is cleared up and we find Irene. She's a friend, you know. Patrick, I hope you find something in the Whitebread house. I'm sure you will. If they let you in."

THE CLAMBAKE

The ATT Pebble Beach Pro-am began in 1937 and was founded by Bing Crosby. PGA Tour pros tee it up with entertainment celebrities and corporate CEOs in a unique golf pro and amateur team format. Crosby was an avid golfer with a two handicap. In 1937, he decided to host his inaugural pro-am invitational event at his home club, Rancho Santa Fe Country Club near San Diego. The idea behind the event was to get leading PGA players to come play with his Hollywood buddies and celebrate after the tournament with a clambake. It was an instant hit with both groups. Sam Snead won the first event and won $500 for his efforts. In contrast the winner of the 2024 Signature Event pockets $3,600,000. After a hiatus for World War II, the Crosby Clambake moved north to the Monterey Peninsula in 1947 where it has been played continuously since then. Crosby died on a golf course in Spain in 1977, but the Crosby Clambake continued on until 1985. Thereafter, AT&T became the title sponsor.

Being a signature event in 2024, the tournament includes the top eighty golfers in the world from the PGA tour, as well as eighty amateurs. In all previous years it included many entertainers, but the decision was made that the entertainers were a distraction because of the importance of the tournament. The business executives and sports stars were still included, but the entertainers, controversially, were not allowed to play.

The Clambake party, scheduled for early Tuesday evening, before the tournament, in the Pebble Beach Room, upstairs in the Lodge, is a can't miss event. It's held early in the evening, because unlike the golf pros of the old Big Crosby tournament, who loved to eat and drink and party into the wee hours, the current pros were early to bed, early to rise. The alcohol consumption among the golf pros was now minimal. The alcohol consumption among the business executives and sports stars, on the other hand, was up considerably.

Almost all the top pros were playing. The recognizable-with-one-name guys: Rory, Scottie, Collin, Max, Xander, Victor, Jordan, Justin, Hideki, Rickie. And the top of the rest: Wyndham Clark, Jason Day, Matthew Fitzpatrick, Tommy Fleetwood, Tony Finau, Justin Rose, Patrick Cantlay.

The Pebble Beach Room held two hundred and fifty, with banquet-style round tables. The outdoor tiled deck, overlooking the eighteenth green at Pebble, was usually busy until dinner service and the entertainment started. Although most were not playing in the event, several entertainers were still planning to be at the Clambake party. For the last several years, most of the singing was by country stars, who also played in the amateur division; Eric Church, Jake Owen, Clay Walker, and Darius Rucker usually each sang a few songs. They were all scheduled to sing, although they wouldn't be playing in the tournament. Longtime ATT amateur golfers, Bill Murray, Ray Romano, and Larry the Cable Guy, were not playing either, but it was a certainty they would be at the party, all attempting to be funny. One of the reasons they weren't allowed to play was that Murray often did antics on the course, and especially at the Clambake, that were borderline obnoxious and inappropriate. Maybe humor would be gone from this year's event. The monetary stakes and Fed Ex points were high.

Sports stars, some current, and some retired, drank and watched with interest; Steve Young, Harris Barton, Josh Allen, Alex Smith, Larry Fitzgerald (with his inflated handicap), Aaron Rodgers, and Buster Posey, all rubbed elbows with CEOs, Presidents, and Owners of many of the largest companies in the U.S. Deals were struck. Friendships were made.

All of the PGA Tour executives were there. With the recent defections of Jon Rahm and a few others to LIV, this tournament had to be a showcase of solidarity and great golf. Nothing could be left to chance and nothing could go wrong.

No wonder security was tight and a priority.

AMIR "WHITEBREAD"

Irene McVay's guest house tenant, known to her as Greg Whitebread, finished his early evening prayers and then slipped on his overalls. The logo on the left chest of the gray overalls said WB Electric, with a few lightning symbols below it. As instructed, he went around to the driveway, out the front gate, and waited a few minutes for the white van that was supposed to pick him up. The van arrived right on time. It had the same WB Electric logo on the side.

Amir entered the passenger side. He had never met the driver before and the Arab man driving didn't give his name. All he said was, "All you need is in the backpack behind your seat. Ladder is in the back. Doors unlocked." Amir reached behind him and was surprised that the backpack was so small. He pulled it onto his lap and opened the backpack. He reached in and, as expected, he found a pin-on name tag, which he put on the right chest area of his overalls. It said "Steve." There was also a cap, with the same logo, which he put on his head. He smiled at the driver. The driver was impassive.

The van negotiated the 17-Mile Drive toward the lodge. It was travelling very slowly. No attention was wanted.

Amir thought to himself, *Tonight is the easy one. I wonder why they are having me do this. I must not ask questions, though. I know how this works.*

Just do your job. Just do your job as planned. This shouldn't take more than twenty minutes.

The van pulled up in front of the Lodge and parked in a red zone. The driver stayed in the car and pulled his WB Electric cap down over his forehead. Amir took the backpack, pulled his cap down, and quickly moved to the back of the van. He opened the doors and took out the metal extension ladder. He closed the doors and walked the short distance to the front door. It was crowded near the front door and in the entrance to the Lodge. No one seemed to even notice him. The two doormen nodded in his direction as he entered the Lodge and walked very slowly to the stairwell in the adjoining corridor to his right. He didn't want to brush anyone with the extension ladder he was carrying.

Amir easily negotiated the steps and found himself on the upper level. A sign said the Pebble Beach Room was to the right. There was one security guard who merely nodded at him. He walked by three metal detector machines that were sitting against the walls but were not operational yet. He tried the first door to the room, and it was locked. The second door was open. He glanced outside and admired the view of the night lights shining on the eighteenth green. The room was already set up for the Clambake party: round tables spread around the large room, tablecloths on all of them but no plates or silverware or glasses. A stage with sound equipment was on one side of the room. Four bars, with dozens of alcohol beverage choices on and behind them, were already set up.

Amir looked up at the twelve-foot ceilings. There were two huge chandeliers in the soffited ceiling. The six smoke detectors were equally spaced, coming out of the soffited part of the ceiling. The associated sprinkler heads were a few feet from each smoke detector. *This is going to be very easy,* he thought to himself. He could tell they were Ionization-type smoke alarms. They have a small amount of radioactive material between two electrically charged plates, which ionizes the air and causes current to flow between the plates. When smoke enters the chamber, it disrupts the flow of ions, thus reducing the flow of current, and activates the alarm.

He also knew that sprinkler systems don't work like in the movies. It is the rare system which is designed to activate more than one sprinkler head simultaneously. The movie scenes where someone, accidentally or purposely, activates dozens of sprinkler heads with gushing water all at the same moment in a huge room is something which Hollywood directors obviously think looks really cool. But they don't operate that dramatically in real life.

Amir, from looking at the plans beforehand, knew that the sprinkler system was a wet one. That means that water is present in the pipes under normal water pressure all the time. Individual sprinkler heads are heat-activated at a specific temperature threshold determined by the needs of that room, its contents, and the relevant fire code. When the head reaches that temperature, a glass vial or soft metal pin which is blocking the stem will melt or break, freeing up a spring, which pushes a small rod and gasket out of the head, opening the tube to water flow.

He didn't have to mess with the smoke detectors, only the sprinkler heads. He stood under the first sprinkler head and extended his ladder. He reached in his backpack and pulled out the first smart button. It had a peel-off sticker on the back. He had worked with these buttons before and was always surprised how small it was. No one would notice. He climbed the ladder, with some trepidation, and applied it to the first sprinkler head. He moved the ladder and applied the buttons to all six sprinklers.

When he was done with all six, he folded the ladder, closed the backpack, and stood in the middle of the large room. He used his cell phone to sync with all six buttons. He heard six little "dings," one at a time. His job was done for the evening. He carried his ladder and backpack out, down the corridor, down the stairs, and put the ladder in the back of the van. His driver smiled at him, his first smile of the evening, and drove Amir back to Irene's estate.

The driver's last words were "See you tomorrow. Same time. Same place."

MONTEREY HERALD

BYLINE DEVINE

PEBBLE BEACH SOCIALITE MISSING

On the eve of the biggest golf week in years on the Monterey Peninsula, added drama has been added with a missing person report filed by William O'Shea regarding wealthy Pebble Beach socialite, Irene McVay. The widow McVay has been missing for four or five days, as reported by O'Shea. Irene McVay is fifty-nine years old.

O'Shea lists himself as a close friend of the missing woman. McVay has an estate off the eleventh fairway at Pebble Beach Golf Course. O'Shea had a scheduled date with McVay at her house and found her car parked in the driveway with her purse and cell phone left in the passenger seat of her vintage Mercedes.

She is a prominent socialite who is often seen playing tennis at the Beach and Tennis Club. She was a regular guest at the Hastings' monthly dinners and has many friends in the Pebble Beach society set. O'Shea says "It isn't like Irene to go missing. She's kind of a homebody and enjoys being in her comfortable home. I and all of her friends are very worried."

At the present time, it seems that the local Monterey County Sheriff's Department is cooperating with the regional FBI office in investigating. Richard Stein, General Counsel of the Pebble Beach Corporation and a friend of Ms. McVay, told this reporter that there are aspects of the case that he cannot divulge at this time. Stein indicated he was the one who asked for FBI involvement.

We will keep following this breaking story and provide follow-ups online as we receive them.

MONTEREY COUNTY WEEKLY

THE SQUIDFRY

WHEN IS SIX HUNDRED FIFTY MILLION NOT ENOUGH?

Squid bait...Is the Squid the only one thinking that there is more to the story of Irene McVay's disappearance than meets the eye? Byline Devine wrote a short piece in the Monterey Herald about the wealthy socialite going missing. Five days and counting now. McVay was often mentioned in the Squidfry. The Squid remembers she once had an affair with the much younger Walter "Chipper" Blair. Yes, THAT Chipper Blair.

About a year ago, Blair was suspected of killing wealthy Scotsman, Ben Morris, when Morris unexpectedly left Blair six hundred and fifty million dollars in his will. Assistant golf pro Blair and his new wife, also an assistant golf pro, live in a multimillion-dollar estate on the fourteenth fairway of Pebble Beach Golf Course.

Blair lived in McVay's guest house before becoming a multimillionaire and, although he was thirty years younger, was having a torrid affair with Irene McVay. Is there no end to the man's depravity? Irene McVay is rumored to be worth two hundred and fifty million and has NO HEIRS. I repeat...HAS NO HEIRS. If McVay never shows up again, it will be interesting to see who she left her money to.

The Squid is on this, like a bear to honey.

HOME INVESTIGATION

After Richard Stein had called the San Francisco Regional FBI office with his report of Irene McVay being missing and his suspicions of the Arabs living in estates, it was taken very seriously. Special Agent in Charge, Robert Tripp, had coordinated with local authorities and was driving to Pebble Beach along with two of his agents, Agustin Lopez and Elvis Chan.

They were to meet Monterey County Sheriff's Deputies Kyle Anderson and Jackson Henderson. Anderson and Henderson were experienced in dealing with Pebble Beach issues and had been involved with Stein and Chipper Blair quite a bit over the past year. They weren't that excited about working with the FBI, but this was an important one. They were scheduled to meet Tripp and his team at the Starbucks in Del Monte Center before heading into Pebble Beach for a surprise search of the Whitebread estate. They were to meet Pebble Beach Security Chief Patrick Black at the estate.

The deputy sheriffs and Special Agent Tripp had spoken on the phone a few times. They had filed probable cause for a search warrant of the Whitebread house and were sitting outside at Starbucks waiting for Tripp. They always felt self-conscious sitting at Starbucks and would have chosen another location to meet, but Tripp was insistent. Tripp was also late. People always misjudged how long it took to get from San Francisco to Monterey.

Anderson and Henderson both were drinking strong black coffee. They were an imposing team sitting in their uniforms. Both big men. Henderson, black with a shaved head. Anderson, white with short dark hair. Both were armed with guns showing. Badges gleaming in the winter sun. When they saw three men walking over from the parking lot in suits and ties, one white, one Asian, and one Hispanic, they were sure it was Tripp, Chan, and Lopez.

Henderson was personable and eager to meet Tripp. Anderson was sullen, as usual. Not eager. Henderson had googled Tripp and found his background extremely impressive. He had a master's and PhD in history. His experience was varied, with work in both California, and Washington D.C.: Intelligence research, Cyber investigations, corporate and securities fraud, public service corruption, civil rights, violent crime, and organized crime. Tripp was thin and fit, middle-aged, about as tall as both Henderson and Anderson, just over six feet. His hair was very short and he was wearing aviator shades. The white shirt and suit and tie would make one think FBI, even if they weren't expecting him.

Elvis Chan, also dressed like Tripp, approached first, and introduced himself. He was wearing shades, balding, and muscular. Much shorter than Tripp. Henderson knew he was an expert in cybercrime and security, cyberterrorism, and had received a master's degree from the Homeland Security Program at the Naval Postgraduate School in Monterey. He was familiar with the area.

Henderson couldn't find much online about Agustin Lopez. All he knew was that Lopez was the criminal branch chief of the San Francisco regional office. He must have spent a lot of time undercover to have so little written about him online. Lopez had a winning smile and longer hair than either Tripp or Chan. He put out his hand toward Anderson first. His grip was vise-like. Anderson had a hard time not wincing.

Tripp, although late, said, "I need a coffee," and went inside. Chan and Lopez sat with Anderson and Henderson. It took a long time for Tripp to come out of the Starbucks. When Anderson saw that the venti coffee he was drinking was some sort of flavored choice, his view of Tripp became even more sullen. Chan was chatting about his time at the Postgraduate School and how much he loved coming to Monterey and Pebble Beach, but when Tripp sat down with his flavored coffee, the discussion turned serious.

Tripp was all business when he said, "This guy Stein that called us seems a bit unhinged. He had some theories that Ms. McVay's disappearance had something to do with a bunch of Arabs planning something bad during tournament week. We don't feel there is any reason to feel that way. The guy was pretty panicked."

Henderson said, "We're very familiar with Richard Stein. We've had a lot of dealings with him. He's a real operator. He knows how to get things done. We've been involved with a lot of incidents in the Forest the last year. Usually Stein and Chipper Blair are in the middle of them."

Tripp said calmly, "I'm speculating here, but Blair, we want to investigate him, too. Quite a bit of history with the missing lady. He always seems to be in the middle of a lot of trouble. Can't keep away from it. Seems to find him coming and going. We definitely want to talk to Blair after we look over the Whitebread house. He's got to be considered a person of interest, based on his background with that Mr. Morris and his past relationship with Irene McVay."

Anderson said, "Don't waste your time. Blair is always just a victim, as well. Nice guy. Just wants to play golf. I can't see him doing anything bad."

"How many people and animals has he hit with his nine iron lately?"

Henderson laughed and said, "I think Chipper would correct you here and say it was his pitching wedge!"

Tripp didn't laugh or even smile. "Not a joking matter, Officer Henderson. Blair seems like a typical con man. Always slithers out of trouble."

The others could tell Anderson was getting impatient. He took out the search warrant and waved it around and said, "Let's get going. Too much talk and not enough activity. What's in that coffee, Agent Tripp?"

"Just enough to get me going, Officer Anderson. Sweet stuff. OK. Let's see what kind of activity you are prepared for. We'll meet you at the house. Do we need to brief you on a thorough house search or are you up on the latest techniques?" This time Tripp laughed in an attempt to exert his influence. Anderson didn't laugh or smile.

"Just let me do the talking when we are there," Tripp said, "Just follow my lead. I don't expect trouble, but keep your weapons at the ready."

In fifteen minutes, they were at the front gate of the Whitebread estate. The FBI car with the three agents was first, and Chan hit the intercom button. Henderson was driving the Monterey County Sheriff's car following. Patrick Black's own sedan was waiting when the other two cars arrived, and he pulled in behind Henderson. Black had a Pebble Beach Security stick-on logo on both the driver's door and the passenger door.

Someone answered the intercom immediately, and Chan said, "FBI. We have a warrant to search your house. Please let us in." There was a buzz on the other end, and a few minutes passed before a man with an accent came on and said, "We were expecting you. We will buzz you in. We have nothing to hide."

All three cars drove through the gate, on the driveway, to near the front door. Each officer had one hand on their hidden guns. Black was unarmed. The six men exited their cars and stepped to the front door.

Hands still on their weapons. An older man with a keffiyeh and white thawb opened the front door and said, "Welcome to my humble home."

Tripp took the search warrant from Anderson and waved it in front of the man and said, "It's not so humble. We have a search warrant. Are you Mr. Whitebread?"

The man said, "Whitebread is just a name we use to keep people from being suspicious of us. I see that it has not helped. My name is Hassan Ahmad." Lopez, Anderson, and Black all had small old-style memo pads that they were using to keep notes. Ahmad saw them scribbling and said, "Here, have my card. It has everything you need to know." He handed a card to each of the six men.

The business card was a golden color and said,

HASSAN AHMAD, VICE PRESIDENT
GOLF SAUDI
PUBLIC INVESTMENT FUND
SOVEREIGN WEALTH FUND

Along with a cell phone number.

Tripp asked, "Why did you say you were expecting us?"

"We are Arabs living in the United States. We always expect you. Even more, we are living in an expensive estate in a white bastion. Why should we not expect you?"

Tripp again held the search warrant out for Ahmad to review, but Ahmad merely said, "I am sure it is in order. I don't have to look at it. We have nothing to hide."

"Do you know Irene McVay?" asked Tripp.

"The name is not familiar to me. Should I?"

"She has been missing for five days, and people are worrying about her. We are examining leads as to where she might be."

"I am not familiar with the woman. Why should she be here?"

115

Tripp continued, "Can you please give me the names of all those living in this house? Not the Whitebread name but their actual names."

"I am the only one that lives here full time. The others are guests for the next week during the golf tournament we are observing. We are all with LIV Golf and are here to learn."

"You purchased the house, correct?"

"I was not involved with the purchase, but yes, the Saudi Investment Fund bought this house as an investment. I am a guest, as well. Nice house, actually. Take a look around."

"Oh. We intend to do that, Mr. Ahmad."

Henderson could tell that Tripp was getting angry. He wasn't expecting Whitebread to be polite. He was expecting some reluctance. The fact that Whitebread wasn't upset meant either he was really good at covering up or, more likely, had nothing to hide. All six investigators headed off in different directions. Within thirty minutes, they had completed a cursory examination of the entire house. Chan had dusted for prints in several rooms and the basement. None of them went in the back yard as the two Dobermans and the Pit bull were wandering around. The house was strangely quiet. All the beds were made. The kitchen had very few items in it, either to eat or to cook with. There were only a few robes hanging in the closets.

After searching and leaving the Whitebread estate, Henderson called Bill O'Shea, and O'Shea met the group at Irene McVay's.

JENNY

Earlier that morning, Chipper's alarm went off, and he reached over for Jenny. When he didn't find her, he sat up and saw her sitting on a chair near the bed. She was weeping. He stayed in bed and said, "What's up?"

Between sobs, Jenny said, "I don't know how you take all this so casually. You never worry about anything."

Chipper just nodded his head. He was impatient to get up and play some golf on his way to Spanish Bay.

Jenny continued, "The damn Squid said you might be responsible for Irene being missing. Can you believe that? On top of everything else. We don't know where Irene is. She might be dead! I know I shouldn't be, but I'm fond of Irene. I hope I'm like her in thirty years. And the SPCA is still on your back for hitting those dogs. And you've been banished to Spanish Bay. While we're at it, I'm afraid that when you finally make the morning shot, you're going to die like Ben did. I'll be all alone in this big house. All those frat boys are still watching me give Cindy lessons every day. I can't go on like this. And you don't seem to mind any of it."

Chipper didn't want to say anything. He kept himself from being silent, though, by trying to calm Jenny down, "Which one of those should I deal with first, Jenny? I do worry about a lot of this stuff, but I'm optimistic it's going to go away. Irene will show up unhurt. I'll be back from Spanish Bay in a week or so. I'm a young man. Ben was an old man.

A very old man. The SPCA guys know what really happened. Do you want me to go over to hit the frat guys with my wedge? I'm good at that!"

Jenny sobbed, "See? You don't take this seriously. You think hitting someone with your wedge will solve everything!" Then she started laughing and came over and gave Chipper a hug. "I miss playing our way into work together, Chipper. I really miss it. I wish you were back at the Pebble driving range."

"Play with me this morning, and I'll drop you off at the Lodge."

"I don't have to be in there so early. It's still dark when you go by there. I'll try to be patient."

"Maybe one of us will hit it in the hole this morning. Then we can make a baby."

"Why don't you just stay in bed with me, and we'll try to make a baby now?" Jenny smiled.

"Tempting, Jen. But I have to get going, or I'll be late."

She said, "Golf over sex again. You are a strange one, Chipper Blair."

Chipper started getting out of bed, and Jenny said, "Just one more thing. Stevens invited me to the big Clambake party in the Lodge on Tuesday night. They want to present me with my Golf Digest teaching award in front of the large group. My friend Kira is playing again, so I'll get to see her."

"Wonderful," Chipper said, "I always wanted to go to that. All the top pros will be there. Remember, your former Miss America friend loves me."

Jenny started sobbing again, "Stevens told me I had to come by myself. I can't bring you. He didn't specifically say 'Don't bring your husband,' he just said that the room size was only big enough for the players, playing amateurs, and a select few other important people. I feel bad about going by myself, without you."

Chipper said, "You have to go, Jenny. It's a big deal. I want you to go. Don't worry about me."

"Worrying about you is how this conversation started, Chipper."

CHIPPER

Chipper dressed quickly and headed out to the back yard. Jenny stayed behind with Angus. Angus still wouldn't go outside. Angus stayed inside, while Jenny, in a warm robe, stood on the deck and watched Chipper take a few warm-up swings, then hit the Slazenger with his long spoon. He said, "I think it's a good one, Jenny."

Jenny looked through the telescopic sight toward the fourteenth green and started jumping up and down, yelling, "It went in, Chipper! It went in! Come back to bed, and we'll make a baby!"

Chipper just yelled, "Nice try, Jenny! Very funny! It's probably about ten feet short and a bit right!" Jenny went inside the house and petted Angus for a long time.

When Chipper got to the fourteenth green, he found his Slazenger exactly where he thought it would be. He thought to himself how lucky he was to be married to Jenny Nelson. He then drove the short distance to the fifteenth tee and turned his tactical flashlight on the highest setting. It was like daylight. He saw a few houselights go on shortly after, on the left side of the fairway. He didn't care. He had missed a few days of early morning golf and was anxious to hit his drive down the fairway. He hit a beauty down the middle with a slight draw.

He kept his light on the whole way down the road to the left of the fairway, around the barranca, and back to the middle of the fairway. He only had seventy-five yards to the green, but the pin was tucked to the back right, over a yawning bunker. If he was in a tournament, he would have played safe to the left, but this morning he took dead aim and hit a great sand wedge to three feet short of the hole. It just hit and bit on the damp green.

As he drove around the green and got out of his cart, he saw a Pebble Beach security guard, now standing a few feet away from his golf cart. The security guard didn't look happy when he said, "What the hell do you think you are doing out here? This is the third morning in a row I had to get up early to try to find the idiot who was making the sky glow and upsetting the homeowners. Just what the hell are you doing?"

Chipper said, "Well, right now, I'm going to make this three-footer for a birdie."

"OK, wise guy. You know what I mean. What the fuck are you doing out here in the dark? What kind of light is that?"

Chipper kept walking toward his ball, and the security guy strolled alongside. Chipper handed him the flashlight. "Take a look," Chipper said. "Just don't shine it in your own eyes or mine." The guard pointed the flashlight up the fifteenth fairway and flicked various buttons and watched the different light patterns.

When the flashlight was on laser, the security guard said out loud, "Damn. Just damn. Look at that. Where can I get one of these?"

Chipper said, "Hit the button one more time, please, and shine it on this putt. What do you think? Going to break a few inches left?"

The security guard said, "It's uphill. I wouldn't play it out of the cup. Just hit it firm a bit right of center."

Chipper smiled and tapped it in easily. "Nice birdie," said the security guard.

Chipper said, "Thank you. I'm not going to play sixteen. I'm headed over to Spyglass. Why don't I shine the light down the sixteenth fairway, and you hit a few with my driver?"

The security guard reached for Chipper's driver and handed the flashlight back. Chipper put it on high and pointed toward the middle of the fairway. It magically was daytime. The guard took a few practice swings. Chipper told him to swing a bit more upright. The guard took a few more swings. Chipper handed him the Slazenger and a tee. "This is unbelievable," said the guard.

His first drive was a weak cut that ended in the right rough about two hundred yards off the tee. Chipper threw him a Titleist and said, "When you head back, just pick up the balls and keep them. I got a hunch you are going to hit a good one." The second drive was hit solidly about two hundred fifty yards right down the middle. Chipper put it on laser light and pointed the light at the ball and yelled, "Right down the middle, sport!"

The guard said, "Thanks. You know I have to report this, because the CEO has his pants on fire about this one. Tournament week starts in just two days. Some pros are already here. I'm not going to take you in. In fact, how about meeting me here tomorrow morning?"

Chipper said, "I'll do you one better. How about meeting me on the fifteenth tee, and we'll play fifteen, and you can hit a few more drives on sixteen again?"

"Sounds great. Thanks for the golf tip. What did you say your name is?"

Chipper just said, "Last name is Whitebread. Just moved in last month, into a house off the fourteenth fairway. Nice to meet you. See you tomorrow."

MORNING MEETING

Donald Stevens opened the morning meeting in a bad mood. "The complaint calls came in again this morning. These homeowners are really angry. I'm really tired of this. I really don't need this at the start of tournament week. I have other things to worry about. The practice rounds start in two days. Pros are in town already. We don't need this…"

Patrick Black interrupted him, "Donald. My guy out on the fifteenth hole this morning found the culprit…"

Stevens stood up and interrupted back, "Why didn't you call me immediately? What is it all about?"

"It's a guy in a golf cart playing early morning golf. He has this military grade special flashlight that lights up the night, so it looks like daylight. My guy couldn't stop talking about the light. He said it was amazing…"

"Well who the hell is it, and do we have him in custody?"

"We don't have any authority to arrest or even detain people…"

"Well, I am now giving you authority to detain whoever it is. Shoot him if you have to. Get him the fuck off my golf course!"

"Very funny, Donald."

"It is not meant to be funny. I want whoever it is off my golf course. Even if it wasn't tournament week, what the hell does this guy think he is doing? And why did we have calls again from Spyglass? This guy is a menace. Who would do this?"

Black said, "The menace told my guy his name was Whitebread. He had just moved in off the fourteenth fairway."

Stevens was still standing and yelled, "Whitebread! Whitebread! Whitebread again! What is it with these people? Did he look Arab?"

"My guy said he was kind of dark. Had a mustache. I asked him if the man looked Arab and he said he couldn't tell. Maybe."

At this point, Richard Stein, who had been listening intently to the interchange, thought to himself. *It's obviously Chipper. Who else would be doing this?* Stein smiled involuntarily and looked at Roger Hennessey, at the other side of the table. Hennessey smiled back and mouthed *Chipper* silently toward Stein.

Stevens told Black. "I want him stopped if he is out tomorrow morning. On the Whitebread situation, Patrick, what's up with investigating them?"

"Yesterday I met three FBI guys and Anderson and Henderson of the sheriff's office, and we did a search of the Whitebread estate. The guy there admitted they just used the name Whitebread as kind of a joke and to avoid suspicious people. His real name is Hassan Ahmad. He is with the LIV group. He's a big shot, clearly. Claims they are just here to observe the golf tournament and learn. We all searched the house and found nothing. He said he was expecting us, because Arabs always are suspect in the U.S. Then we all went to the McVay estate and looked around her house too. Didn't find any reason there for her being missing."

Stevens asked, "Did the FBI guys indicate any worries about the Arabs?"

"They play it pretty close to the vest. These guys are hard to read."

Stevens pulled out a copy of the Monterey Weekly and asked, "Anyone see the Squid column?"

Some had read it, but no one nodded or said they had. Stein was ready for what was coming next.

"Squid suspects Chipper Blair. I'm glad we got him off the payroll."

He looked at Hennessey and got no reaction at all. "I've had enough for this morning. This isn't what I wanted to discuss in this meeting. This will be our last meeting because we all have a ton to do during tournament week. I'll see you all at the Clambake party on Tuesday evening. We have a Corporation table near the front. I want everyone to wear suits and their name tags. And don't drink too much."

RICHARD STEIN

Richard Stein was upset with the lack of progress in finding Irene McVay. He kept calling FBI agent Tripp, as well as Henderson and Anderson, and his own head of security, Patrick Black. There didn't seem to be a sense of urgency. He was repeatedly told they were doing all they could with the investigation. Stein decided to take matters into his own hands and drove over to his estate that was now rented by another group headed by a Mr. Whitebread.

He had been unable to get in to inspect since they paid for their short term rental. The code numbers were changed on the front gate lock. *Why don't these agents get a warrant to search my house?* He thought to himself. Stein pulled up to the gate and pushed the call button and was surprised when a voice answered quickly.

"This is Richard Stein. You are in my house and I demand to enter. You have to let me in to look at my house. NOW!"

There was silence on the other end. Stein waited several minutes and pushed the call button again. No one answered this time. He exited his car and stood at the gate and looked toward the driveway but couldn't see anything. He called Special Agent Tripp.

"Tripp. This is Stein. I am in front of my house, and I cannot get in to inspect it. The Arabs in there have changed the locks. I have told you this before! There has to be something you can do!"

"I told you, Stein. We have no reason to search that house. There is no cause. We can't get a warrant."

"Tripp. You are useless. Of course there is cause. They are connected to the other Whitebreads. They are all together. Irene McVay may be in my house right now. Isn't that reason enough?"

"Your suspicions are not reason for a warrant. They haven't done anything. We were able to get a warrant for the other house because Ms. McVay was known to have gone there. We have no such reason for your house."

Stein was yelling now, "What if I tell you I told her to come over here, just as I told you about the other house?"

"Don't yell at me, Stein! I wouldn't believe you. I am convinced the Whitebreads or whatever they call themselves are not hiding Irene. We checked out Hassan Ahmad, and his story checks out. He is with the Saudi group, and all of these people are here legitimately to observe the golf tournament. That's all they are here for. You should talk to your friend Blair about where Irene McVay is. He is definitely a person of interest here. Just go back to work and do what you do. Whatever that is? Stay out of this. We are on top of it. We'll have some evidence pretty soon to arrest Blair." Then Tripp hung up.

Stein was livid. He started yelling through the gate, "Let me in! Let me in!" And started pounding on the iron gate until his hands hurt. He went back and kept pressing the button. No one answered.

SPANISH BAY FIRST TEE

Chipper had a few minutes between foursomes and was hitting some drivers down the first fairway. He was pretending he was playing in the ATT and giving first tee player announcements for himself. In his mind, he was leading with one round to go. *Now hitting is the third round leader, Mr. Chipper Blair. Play away.* He waved to the imaginary crowd. Took a few practice swings. Hitched up his pants. Waved to the crowd again. Stood behind the ball to get a good line. Stepped up to the ball and hit a solid one right down the middle. He announced, *Blair hits one right down the middle. You would think he would be nervous, but he seems well in control of his emotions and his golf ball.* Then he imagined the crowd going wild. He waved one last time.

The day was pretty uneventful in the morning for Chipper. Midafternoon, the fog started rolling in, and the wind picked up. He was happy he had a tent for protection from the elements. A foursome of cigar-smoking, middle-aged men were walking to the tee, after parking their carts close by. Chipper was admiring their plaid shorts and wondering why tourists who come to the Del Monte Forest to play golf don't realize how cold it can be all year round, especially in late January. He was surprised at himself for having some empathy and said, "Hello, gentlemen. You might want to put on some longer pants, and windbreakers. It's gonna be cold out there."

One of the men said, "We weren't planning for this at all. Is it always this cold and windy?"

Chipper smiled and said, "Most of the time. By the time you are a few holes out, you won't be able to see because of the fog, and it will be windier and colder. Damp, too. You have time to go inside and buy some gear to keep you warmer."

"Not at these prices. We'll tough it out, I guess," said another of the men. He had goosebumps already and was shaking.

Another, who was trying to relight his stogie said, "Where do we hit it here?"

Chipper replied, "Right down the middle is always best. Very wide fairway. You'll find a few Titleists out there that I just hit. Just put them in your bag and keep them. My gift to you. Stay moving to keep warmer. Try to have fun. Where are you from?"

"South Carolina. We're here to play a few days and then watch the golf tournament."

"You might want to buy some warmer clothes, then. Might be like this all next week."

Chipper watched them hit and did commentary on each in his head, *Up steps shivering man number one. It's a tough day out here, all you golf fans. And it's only gonna get tougher. Shivering man has a decent swing, but a reverse weight shift. He hits it about one hundred and seventy yards down the right side of this wide fairway. Up steps his playing partner. A very portly man, and I am being polite. Very portly. His practice swing indicates he's been portly for a long time as it's a grooved very flat swing. I am predicting a low hook. AND I AM CORRECT! It's about two hundred yards down the left side. Going to be a very long day for these men.*

Chipper retreated to his tent to watch the next two, but he noticed that three men in suits were walking toward the tee. He stayed in the tent and couldn't continue his play-by-play in his mind. The first man said, "Are you Walter Blair?"

"Yes, I am." Chipper then remained silent.

"My name is Special Agent Tripp from the San Francisco office of the FBI." He then flashed his wallet showing his I.D. card at Chipper. Chipper didn't even have time to look at it before the man slipped it back in his coat pocket. Tripp then pulled his suit jacket back so Chipper could see the pistol in his holster on his hip. Chipper wasn't impressed.

Tripp continued, "We are here to investigate the missing person report for Ms. Irene McVay. Am I correct that you know her?"

"Yes. She is a good friend. We all have been very worried about her."

"How good a friend? As we understand it, you and Ms. McVay had an affair a short time ago."

"I would call it an arrangement rather than an affair. I lived in her guest house, and she gave me free rent for doing odd jobs at her house and other services."

"She is thirty years older than you, correct?"

"Also correct," was all Chipper said. Tripp waited for more of an explanation.

Tripp, after a long pause, said, "Blair. Do you know where she is?"

Chipper was getting impatient as he saw another group of golfers coming to the tee. "Of course I don't know where she is. We all suspect that she went to the Whitebread house next door to mine, and they have her somewhere. We think they are up to something."

Chipper started to walk out of the tent to help the next group, but Tripp moved in front of him in a confrontational way. Chipper walked around him. Tripp came out of the tent and walked up to the golfers and showed his FBI I.D. and said, "Mr. Blair can't help you now. Just go ahead and tee off."

Chipper's patience was on a slow burn. "Please get on with this, Tripp. What can I do for you, then?"

"You have a very expensive estate here. How does a guy, who stands on the tee and helps people play golf, afford such a home?" Chipper saw the other two agents smile at the question.

"You already know, no doubt, that I inherited the estate."

"And you also know that Irene McVay is worth millions and has no heirs, right?"

Chipper now was full-out angry and shouted, "You know I know that she's worth millions. I loved Irene McVay. I would never hurt her. You are barking up the wrong tree!"

'No reason to get upset, Blair. We're going to find her will and see who she left her money to. Are you afraid of that? Do you need another two or three hundred million bucks?"

Chipper was silent. Now Tripp was angry and shouted back, "Don't leave town, Mr. Blair! We know your kind! We'll find that will. We searched the Whitebread house and the McVay house and found nothing suspicious. The Arabs are just here to observe the golf tournament. They have nothing to gain by hiding Irene McVay. Certainly, they don't need ransom money. They have even more money than you do. Don't leave town, Blair!"

Chipper watched them walk away.

IRENE MCVAY

Irene McVay didn't know whether it was day or night in the wine cellar, or how many days she had been in it. She turned the lights on when she felt like it but kept them off most of the time and tried to sleep. She was hoping sleep would cure the pains in her side and in her head. When she stood up, she was dizzy, so she spent most the time lying down.

She remembered men coming into the wine cellar what seemed like several days ago and kicking her again and then taking several bottles of wine out. They left a package of pita bread that she was trying to ration, as she didn't know when they would come back. Irene did find several bottles that had screw tops, and she didn't remember drinking them, but there were a few empty bottles near her. She looked at them curiously, like they were put there by someone else. She didn't remember drinking any wine.

When the men were standing over her, all she remembered was the kick to the ribs again and the few English words she could understand. "Clambake soon" was one phrase. One man pointed at her and laughed and said "Khashoggi" again. When she slept, she woke up screaming when she pictured the men cutting Jamal Khashoggi into pieces. The nightmare seemed very real. *I hope they just kill me first quickly, before they cut me into dog meat. Why are they waiting so long?* she thought to herself. She woke up screaming and found herself instinctively drinking several gulps of red wine from an open bottle sitting on the floor next to her. She continued to scream until she tired and fell asleep again. *My friends have to be looking for me by now.*

She turned the light on and examined herself. There was no mirror, but she could see that her clothes, still the tennis outfit, were tattered and very dirty. She felt her face and her side and found both swollen. *I look a mess. I'm a beast. When will Big Bill come busting through the door and save me? Damn that man. Oh, now I'm talking to myself out loud. I have to do something. I have to clean up.* She started screaming again and drinking more wine.

I have to get out of here. I have to do something. Be strong, Irene. You have always been strong. Be strong. Those men aren't going to come and save me. I have to do this myself. I need a plan. I need a plan. Irene started screaming again and pounding on the wine cellar door until she fell to the floor and passed out.

When she awoke, she went to the champagne section and grabbed three bottles of Dom Perignon. She sat them upright on the floor, just to the right of the door. Then Irene McVay slid down the wall slowly, next to the bottles, and with her back supported by the wall, sat and waited. She tried to stay awake.

AMIR WHITEBREAD

This was going to be a long and potentially dangerous night for Amir. He was expecting the van outside the security gates at the estate at seven PM. He wasn't notified as to what to wear, so he put on the same WB Electric overalls he had worn a few days before. Tonight's mission was potentially much more dangerous.

The driver pulled up a few minutes late. It was a different driver than last time. Amir didn't know this person, either. All the wheel man said was, "Get in the back and put on a different outfit. It is waiting. Don't touch anything else. Don't touch anything but the uniform."

Amir exited the passenger seat and went behind the van. He entered the back of the van and saw the uniform hanging up. There was also a metal container taking up half of the rest of the van. He examined the uniform and saw that the logo this time was both on the pants and top of the overalls. They both said THRIFTY PEST CONTROL in block letters. Underneath each was a bug that looked like a beetle lying on its back. Obviously dead. He shed his one uniform and carefully and deliberately put on the new one. "Hurry up, back there!" shouted the driver.

When he was back in the passenger seat, the driver turned on the engine and drove deliberately out the gate and toward Spanish Bay. He said in a low voice, "Make sure you put on the protective gloves and headgear before you pick up the canister. Lift it carefully, release the wheels, and roll it carefully into the Inn."

"I know all this already," said Amir.

"My instructions are to remind you. Just following my instructions. You know Hassan. Everything has to be checked and double-checked. The canister is just a container. It has no purpose, other than to look like a bug spray device. When inside, just slide the bottom off, and all you need is in the canister. Very dangerous stuff. Very dangerous."

"I know all that," Amir said impatiently. Amir didn't tell the driver that he had gone against Hassan Ahmad's instructions and had actually had a conversation with the man they all just called, "The Chemist." The Chemist was living and working in the estate next to Chipper's until about a week before. He was done with his work and left the house immediately after that.

Amir knew that what the Chemist was working on was in the canister Amir was entrusted to tonight. The fatal cocktail of drugs included illicitly manufactured fentanyl, a methamphetamine, and high concentration hydrogen cyanide gas. Since the cyanide gas was known for an awful smell, the Chemist had mixed in a masking agent that was a mixture of Chanel N°5 and what Ahmad had told him was the main course at the Clambake dinner: rosemary chicken. The smell in the air, when the drugs were released in the ballroom, would blend right in with the dinner service. Exposure was needed for at least thirty minutes to take effect. The results would be catastrophic to everyone in the room. Amir smiled at the ingenuity. He wasn't sure why Hassan Ahmad wanted everyone in the room killed, but he thought it had to do with something about making the LIV Golf group the only one in the world. The profits would be enormous. *Who the fuck cares about golf anyway,* he thought to himself.

The van pulled up to the classy traffic circle in front of the Lodge at Spanish Bay. Amir circled to the back of the van, opened the back doors, and carefully opened the metal box inside. He took out the canister, carried it out of the van, and carefully folded down the wheels. He put on his protective gloves and grabbed the extension ladder hanging on the van wall. Amir walked back to the driver's side of the van and said he would meet the driver in the same place in exactly five hours. They nodded at each other. The driver didn't say a thing, and Amir thought to himself, *he could have at least wished me good luck.*

Amir carefully rolled the canister with one hand and carried the extension ladder in the other arm. He walked very slowly into the lodge and headed to the elevator. No one said anything to him. He knew where the elevator was and got in with another couple. Amir tried not to look at them. The man said, "Does the Inn have pests?" Amir did not reply and pressed the M for the Mezzanine floor.

He found himself in what was called the Ballroom Gallery, a very wide and very long hallway area that could also be used as a function location. There were tables, chairs and bars all stacked up neatly near the walls. Amir was nervous as he tried the first door he came to. It didn't open. He walked a bit and tried another with the same result. The same again. Finally the fourth door opened, and he quickly closed it behind him.

The Grand Ballroom looked exactly like he expected it to look. None of the sliding panels that could separate the ballroom into smaller rooms were up. The room could hold eight hundred people and was the largest of the ballrooms in any of the Pebble Beach Corporation properties. The carpet was the same as the Ballroom Gallery outside: an ornate busy pattern that repeated three times. There were a dozen huge chandeliers that didn't really complement the wood paneled walls. It was an enclosed space with no windows or outlets to the outside. No connecting decks or outside access. He counted seven double doors.

Amir walked to one corner of the huge room and rolled his canister, still carrying the extension ladder. He extended the ladder so he could easily reach the twelve foot ceiling. *This was not going to be difficult, just time consuming,* he thought. He started humming to himself. Amir laid the canister on its side on the carpet and slid open the panel on the bottom. He put the hood of the overalls, which was hanging behind his neck, over his head. It wasn't a usual hoodie, as it buttoned in the front, leaving a plastic panel in front of his face that he could see through.

He carefully took out sixteen small metal containers and left four of them on the floor of the corner he was in. He took another four and walked to the far corner of the ballroom and deposited them on that floor. Then he separately took four more and put them in the opposite corner, the last four going in the one remaining corner.

In the canister were two Phillips screwdrivers; one was a backup. Amir climbed the ladder and took out two of the four screws that held the first heating vent in place. He tilted it down, went down the ladder, and grabbed one of the little metal containers. He very deliberately climbed the ladder again, being careful to make sure he had a good foothold on each rung. When he reached the rung he needed, he unscrewed the top of the metal container and took out a little packet of the concoction the Chemist had put together. It was a powder inside of what looked like a very thin plastic film. The Chemist had told Amir that the plastic film would dissolve at a temperature of seventy-four degrees, and the powder would be distributed in the room by the heating vents.

Amir placed the plastic bag in the heating vent and then replaced the two screws he had taken out. He looked at his watch and was happy to see that the process had taken less than eighteen minutes. He had fifteen more vents to work on in his five-hour estimate for the process to be done. He kept track of his time and finished all sixteen vents in four hours and forty-five minutes. No one came in the room. He took a deep breath when he was done. He was alive. Any accident with the handling of the chemicals, and he wouldn't have been.

Now he had one more task, only in the Grand Ballroom. He proceeded to put a small sensor on each of the three thermostats and sync the sensors to his cell phone, just as he had synced the sprinklers in the ballroom at the Lodge at Pebble Beach.

Amir replaced the bottom of the canister and rolled it with confidence to the elevator. He had the extension ladder in his other arm. When he got in the elevator, he hesitated before getting in, as there was another couple in the elevator. The man said, to him, "Does the Inn have pests?" Amir stayed out of the elevator and waited for the next one.

The van was waiting outside. Amir put the ladder and canister in the back. No worries this time about being careful. The driver didn't say a word until they were at the turnoff to Irene McVay's estate, then the driver said, "Hassan wants to see you," and drove to the house next to Chipper's. Amir was expecting a celebration and maybe a large suitcase full of cash, as per his verbal contract with Hassan. Amir was very tired and ready for bed.

The driver stayed in the van when Amir walked to the front door. It was open, and Hassan and several others were standing in the foyer. Hassan said, "It all went well?"

Amir barely had time to say "Yes" when Hassan Ahmad pulled out his revolver and shot Amir between the eyes. Ahmad then walked over and pulled Amir's cell phone out of his overalls pocket and smiled.

Ahmad said, "Khashoggi him!"

REBECCA SLOANE

Assistant D.A. Rebecca Sloane called Chipper Blair's cell phone number. She almost had it memorized. Chipper was on the tee at Spanish Bay, working. When he answered she said, "Hi, Chipper. How is Jenny?"

"She's fine. How are you, Rebecca? I'm almost afraid this is about the dogs."

"It is about the dogs, but first I wanted to tell you I was visited yesterday by a few FBI guys. They looked like FBI guys. Very strange. You would think they would dress up in some sort of other outfit. They look like adults who dress up like FBI guys for Halloween..." She paused, then continued, "The head guy was asking all sorts of questions about our dealings with you over the past year. I told him you were never convicted of anything, but if bad luck was a crime you would be convicted of having very bad luck."

"Thank you, Rebecca."

"He asked me who was the attorney for Ben Morris' will and I told him Judith Hitten. Then he asked me if I thought she was Irene McVay's attorney, and I told him I didn't know. I called Judith and told her she might get an unexpected visit from them. She confirmed to me that she is Irene's attorney, as well. Irene switched to her after they met at your house."

"OK. Why are you telling me all this?"

"I thought you should know. Aren't you worried?"

"Not particularly. I am worried about Irene. I'm pretty sure the Arabs have her. I hope she is still alive, but I really doubt it at this point. It's just all so bizarre."

"It's been a week now," Sloane commented, "I'm surprised the FBI is concentrating on you, rather than the Whitebreads. Strange name for them."

Chipper didn't want to take the time to explain the Whitebread name to her. He just wanted to get off the phone and back to only golf. He was silent and waited for Sloane to continue.

She said, finally, "I have worked out a plea deal with the SPCA for you…"

Chipper interrupted, "But I haven't done anything. I'm not guilty of anything."

"Don't forget the dogs are dead…"

He stopped her again, "The Whitebreads killed the dogs. I didn't kill the dogs. I was just protecting Angus. He's still traumatized, poor guy."

"Well, Chipper, it isn't clear whether you killed the two dogs or not. You don't want to go to court on this and be convicted of a felony. You admitted you hit the dogs. It won't look good for you in court. If you plead no contest, you'll still get a criminal record, but it won't cost you any money…"

"I don't want a criminal record, and I don't care about the money," said Chipper. "Does paying a bunch of money get me out of this?"

"The SPCA will completely drop the charges against you if you make a rather large donation to the SPCA."

"How large? And what about the charges against the idiots next door who actually killed the dogs?"

"A Mr. Ahmad came in yesterday with a suitcase full of cash and signed some papers. The charges against them have been dropped. He was a very polite man."

"Did you ask him what he has done with Irene?"

"Chipper. Chipper. Chipper. Mr. Ahmad donated two million in cash to the SPCA."

"You've got to be kidding me. That's blackmail. It seems the SPCA can just bring animal abuse or cruelty charges against anyone and then wait for a donation. I won't give two million to them. That's blackmail!"

Sloane said, "How about one million?"

"Do you get a cut, Rebecca?"

"Chipper. I'm surprised at you. You know me. I love the law almost as much as you love golf."

"I doubt that, Rebecca. OK. I have to go. Why don't you come out here? Or send someone to get my signature, and I'll call Judith and tell her to send a check for one million, from the Trust account, to the SPCA as a donation."

"Technically, it has to come from your own account, Chipper."

"What difference does it make? Money is money. It just gives me headaches."

"Tell her to write the check from your own funds, Chipper."

"Goodbye, Rebecca. Really great hearing from you."

Chipper immediately called Judith Hitten and told her to write a donation to the SPCA from his own personal account.

Judith said, "What a wonderful man you are, Chipper. What a lovely donation. I know how much you love Angus. How is Angus?"

"I don't have time to talk now, Judith. Thank you."

"Wait a minute, Chipper. I was going to call you. I had an Agent Tripp visit me today. He knew I helped Irene McVay with her will. He wanted to know if you were in any way a beneficiary. I told him, under attorney-client privilege that I could not tell him. And I can't tell you, either. It's between me and Irene. I hope she gets located soon. Tripp was obnoxious but I stood my ground. He obviously thinks you killed Irene. I told him you would never do that."

"Thanks, Judith. I have to go."

Chipper then dumped every golf ball out of his bag, about a dozen, and started hitting drives down the first fairway.

MONDAY MORNING

Chipper and Jenny were up early. It was finally the week of the ATT Signature Event. The pros and amateurs, many of them celebrities, would all be in town, playing practice rounds at Pebble and Spyglass. Jenny had some lessons scheduled with celebrities and corporate royalty most of the day on Monday, Tuesday, and Wednesday. One of the perks that the Corporation gave to some of the celebrities was free lessons. Jenny would get paid but only by the Corporation. She dressed in baggy clothes, put on a golf cap, and didn't use makeup, so she wouldn't look as attractive as usual. She didn't want to get hit on.

Chipper didn't have to ask her when she wore the baggy clothes. He knew what was going on, and he loved her for it. She still looked great, even trying not to. Both were looking forward to some early morning holes, as it was finally a day that Chipper could drive Jenny into work, and they could play some golf on the way in. He tried to figure out what to say to the security guard that was scheduled to meet him on the fifteenth tee. He could probably introduce her as Mrs. Whitebread, but the guard might recognize Jenny from seeing her around the Lodge and at Spyglass giving lessons.

Poor Angus didn't get out of bed. They covered him with blankets and left him lying on Jenny's pillow. When they descended to the back lawn there was a slight drizzle. It wasn't a pleasant morning. Based on

ATT weather, it was probably going to be miserable all week. Rain was predicted and cold temperatures. It would make sense to move the tournament to September or October, but that would never happen: too much tradition. Some of the players actually looked forward to what was called Crosby weather.

Jenny put on a windbreaker before going outside. She took the morning shot first. Chipper used the tactical flashlight to light up the night. They heard the three remaining dogs next door barking wildly, and they both imagined poor Angus ducking further under the covers upstairs in the bed. Lights went on in the Whitebread house.

After a few practice swings, Jenny hit a mediocre shot that she knew missed the green on the right. Well short of pin high, as well. She showed her disgust. Chipper was going to win this morning's battle, and he knew it. He was feeling good and hit his long spoon about ten feet to the right of the hole, exactly the right distance. As they headed toward the fourteenth fairway to drive his cart to the green, Jenny had to get out of the cart and lift the gallery ropes that had been put in place the day before. It was going to be a pain getting through the Pebble and Spyglass holes because of the gallery ropes.

Just when Chipper drove under the rope that Jenny was holding up, they heard a yell from the Whitebread back lawn. Chipper shined his flashlight in that direction, and the man shielded his eyes with his forearm. He started yelling wildly, "The only good neighbors are dead neighbors. Dead neighbors don't bother us. We know the girl is Jewish. We KNOW!" Chipper took the flashlight, switched to laser bright mode, and aimed at the man's eyes, but he turned away and headed back to the house.

Jenny said, "Fuck him. What a great way to start the day. We have to find a way to get them out of that house."

Chipper put his arm around her damp windbreaker and hugged her before they continued up the fairway. Waiting on the fifteenth tee, was the security guard, and he had his own clubs on the back of the cart. He greeted Chipper with a warm smile, and Chipper introduced Jenny as his wife. The guard said, "You look familiar, ma'am. Whitebread, I saw your light coming up. Where can I get me one of those?"

Chipper replied, "Just go to the Army-Navy surplus store on Broadway in Seaside. It's pretty cheap, really."

"I might buy two, then," he said.

Jenny was stepping up to the men's tees and already teeing it up. When she hit one about two hundred and forty yards down the middle, the security guard yelled, "Mrs. Whitebread can play! Wow! She should turn pro. I've never seen a woman hit one like that." The guard hit next and hit a pretty good one, but it was about twenty yards short of Jenny. Chipper hit three-metal to play for position and was about the same distance as the security guard. Jenny had to again get out of the cart and lift the gallery ropes twice for both of them to get back to the fairway. The lights were on in the three houses on the left.

Jenny whispered to Chipper, "I bet I don't hear anything about being Jewish from those houses! Maybe they want us dead for waking them up, though."

Chipper hit it ten feet from the hole and made birdie. Jenny was just short, chipped up, and made a three footer for par. The security guard was happy with bogey. They all headed to the sixteenth tee, and Jenny said, "Let me give you some pointers on your swing here. You can hit several and see how it goes."

After his first swing, Jenny told him to take it back a little slower and make sure to get set at the top of the backswing. After the second drive, she told him to set up a little more closed to the line of intended flight. That was all the advice the security guard needed. He hit five more drives, all but one of them in the fairway, and about twenty yards further than his drive on fifteen. Chipper said, "We have to go this way again. Have fun out there."

The security guard winked and said, "Thank you for the lesson, miss. You should be a teaching pro." Then he took off down the fairway with his new swing and added confidence with the driver.

"Well, you made someone happy already this morning, and it's not even six thirty yet," Chipper said.

Jenny replied, "I am really good at what I do. Really good. That made me feel good. Although I feel like a wet goose. I'm going to have to towel dry when I get to Spyglass. Maybe some of my lessons will cancel." Chipper headed the cart out to the 17-Mile Drive in the direction of Spyglass Hill. There was already a lot of traffic on the road, most likely people coming to gallery the practice rounds. There would be a lot of sloppy pants by the end of the day. The rain was coming down much harder now.

When he dropped Jenny off at Spyglass, Chipper almost decided to just drive to work and forget the extra holes. Almost. He played ten, eleven, and twelve at Spyglass with his flashlight before the sun finally appeared. Lights flashed on in most of the houses along the fairways. He didn't care.

GIL HANSE

It was a very wet morning at Spanish Bay. Chipper hid under his tent. Didn't even venture out to hit any drivers down the fairway. There were only two foursomes that showed up before 11 AM. Chipper fondly remembered all the times, when he was a kid and in college, when he wouldn't miss a day. No matter how bad the weather was. No matter how hard it was raining. No matter how blustery the wind was. Some days he was the only one he could see playing on Stanford Golf Course.

A bit after 11, Gil Hanse walked up wearing a heavy jacket and rubber boots. Chipper said, "Welcome back. It doesn't look like you are here to play golf."

Hanse said, "We just finished our last tour of the course. I'd like to show you our plans for every hole before I present them to CEO Stevens and the design committee. Can you come in to the clubhouse and meet our group at the Sticks restaurant at noon? We'll grab a bite to eat and take a quick look at the proposed layout and changes. I'd like your opinions."

Chipper was overwhelmed that Hanse would ask for his advice. Hanse was the best in the business. "I'd like to do that, but I'm supposed to stay on the tee until 3 PM. I'd really like to do that."

Hanse said, "No one is going to come out and play now. I'll go inside and talk to your boss. Just assume I've arranged permission and meet us at noon."

Chipper said, "I would go out and play if I could. I've played in a lot worse. Much worse."

"I kind of figured you would. That's why I value your opinion, Chipper. See you inside in a bit."

In the Sticks restaurant, Chipper was surprised that he was meeting only with Hanse. There were no other of his experts and assistants there. The restaurant only had one other table occupied. Hanse had his laptop open and a sheaf of rolled-up architectural plans on the floor next to him. For some reason, Chipper found himself wanting to impress Gil Hanse. He rarely had that feeling. No matter what he did, he couldn't impress his own father. In fact, most of the time, he felt like his father thought he was a disappointment. He really didn't care anymore what his father or anyone else felt. He was comfortable in his own skin. But he did want to impress Gil Hanse.

They started by ordering. Hanse ordered four pulled pork sliders, and some tater tots. Also, an Irish coffee. He said, "Great day for Irish Coffee." Chipper followed and ordered a bowl of chili and a turkey avocado BLT. Then he ordered a Nutty Irishman. "Great day for a Nutty Irishman," Chipper said.

Hanse started, "I know your story, Chipper. Richard Stein told me about your inheritance. I admire you for setting up the foundation and for your love of golf. That Stein seems to be a resourceful fellow. He got permission for some of the environmentally sensitive areas to be reinspected and diminished. It made the remodel of the golf course a lot easier."

Chipper didn't respond but did think to himself, *Richard probably paid off a lot of people to get that done.*

Hanse flipped the laptop screen over toward Chipper and said, "We've created photos of each hole on the new course as we plan it. We are using some new AI technology, and even developing some ourselves, which is quite creative. Look at these pictures." Hanse then clicked through each of the 18 holes very quickly. Chipper couldn't even examine each one in any detail, because they went by so fast.

"Can you go slower, so I can see each one?"

"We'll do that after lunch." Hanse spread out a large plan showing the entire golf course on the table next to them. Chipper took one quarter of his BLT in his hand and stepped over to look at it. Hanse said excitedly, "Don't get any avocado on that!"

While Chipper was surveying the plans, Hanse continued talking, "We followed the basic philosophy that you talked about when we met. It's supposed to be a links golf course. We are going to flatten the terrain as much as we can. Have you ever played Royal Birkdale? We are going to route the course through dunes, so the high points will be dunes off the fairways, rather than the way the greens are now elevated on some holes. We will have a signature hole on each nine that is the most memorable. Holes ten through fourteen now are mostly forest holes, completely different than the linksland concept. We are going to keep the design on those holes but take down many trees and make them look like links holes rather than forest holes. Stein helped us with permits for tree cutting as well. One of the most difficult design aspects was adding five hundred yards in some way. Now the course is only a bit over sixty-seven hundred yards from the blues and the Corporation wants it to be a true test, possibly U.S. Open someday. We are adding yardage here and there to make it almost seventy-three hundred yards from the back. Don't get any avocado on that! We tried to make more holes run toward the ocean, so the view was outstanding. We took out the strange strategic doglegs that, for some reason, Watson liked, but nobody else did. Watch out for that avocado, Chipper!"

Chipper said, "I see you have a short par three near the water that I think is a good one. Eager to see the photos. You've got a late hole strategic, and maybe penal, short par four that every announcer on TV thinks is required these days. I like the fact that the par threes are all different lengths. Hate it when you have to hit the same club on even two of the four par threes. It looks like the short one might be a wedge, and the longest one even a long hybrid for most pros. Love that. Looks like two of the par fives are really three-shotters. But it's hard to tell from this map. Show me the holes on the screen already."

Hanse laughed, "Let's eat lunch first. Your chili is going to get cold. Your comments have made me feel good so far. Are you going to the Clambake party tomorrow? Our whole team will be there. Maybe you can sit with us?"

Chipper said, "Not invited. Stevens doesn't like me at all. My wife will be there. She's getting some sort of teaching pro award. She was in Golf Digest's list of best teachers in the country. And she is. She's great. Stevens made sure to tell her she was invited but only her. She can't bring me."

"I'll make sure to talk to her. Stein told me about her, too. Maybe I'll take a lesson. I don't have much time to play these days. I need a swing that holds up without me playing a lot. The Clambake is going to be great. I've never been to one. Entertainers, business men, the top golfers in the world. I'm really looking forward to it."

Chipper grinned, "Don't make me feel bad."

When they finished lunch, Hanse stood behind Chipper, and they went slowly through every hole and what the design thoughts were. Chipper learned a lot from Hanse. He already knew it was difficult to create a course that would appeal to a top-notch touring pro but that a hack would also enjoy and could play without losing a ton of balls and without needing six hours to play. He learned a lot about drainage issues, keeping maintenance costs down, and creating at least four possible pin positions on each hole by properly contouring the greens. Chipper and Hanse bonded over a hatred of in-course out of bounds; there should never be any. The pictures of each hole were impressive. The new design was impressive. The thought process that went into each hole was obvious. Chipper felt that he should make some recommendations but only said, "I want to play on the first day, please."

At the end, Hanse said, "You know, Chipper. Stein told me your background. You are a smart guy. I've enjoyed my conversations with you. I know you love just being on the driving range, but how would you like to work for me in some capacity? Not full time but when we want your input on things about a golf course design. You could still live here. You might have to travel a bit when we need you."

Chipper was speechless and just shook Hanse's hand without a word.

"Is that a yes?" Hanse finally said.

"It's a maybe. Let me talk to Jenny and think about it awhile. I could still keep my job here at the range, I hope?"

"Yes, we can do that. I assume salary doesn't mean anything to you?"

"Also correct. Money has no meaning for me anymore, either," Chipper said emphatically.

CLAMBAKE PARTY MORNING

Chipper was up early on Tuesday of tournament week. Jenny and Angus were still asleep, and Chipper smiled as he saw her arm was draped over Angus. He thought to himself, *It appears someone has taken my place as favorite bedmate.* He walked to the window and looked out over what he knew should be a view of the fourteenth fairway at Pebble and saw nothing but fog and drizzle again. It was another miserable morning. He had mixed feelings about the weather. On the one hand, he wanted it to be nice for their morning shot, but he felt good that the pros and wealthy amateurs were going to have to deal with bad weather all week. *Nay wind. Nay Rain. Nay Golf.*

He sat near the bed and stared at Jenny and Angus for about ten minutes until the alarm went off. Jenny opened her eyes and looked at Chipper sitting next to the bed. "You love me, don't you? You look jealous of Angus!"

"I am jealous of Angus."

"Let's put Angus in the other room tonight, and when I come home from the Clambake party, we can have our own party."

"That sounds good to me," Chipper agreed.

"Can you do me a favor, Mr. Chips?"

"It depends what it is."

"I'm agonizing over what to wear tonight. Can you drive to work and then come home right after you get off, so I can try some outfits on and get your opinion?"

"That's asking a lot, Jenny. I'm sure you're going to look good in anything you put on."

"You don't understand how difficult this is. I have to look great but still be professional, and still look sexy. Anyone and everyone in the golf world are going to see me when I get my award. And I have to impress Max Homa and Rory. My two crushes."

"That's the first you've said anything to me about that. Why Max and Rory?"

"Well, Rory because he is Rory. And Max, of course, because he's Jewish. And he has great social media. I'm excited to meet him. And my Special K will be there too."

"You could wear a burlap sack and still look sexy. What if Kira K. gets excited and calls you Shoshy again?"

"I hope she does in front of Max. Maybe we'll give each other the secret Jewish handshake."

Chipper played along, "Show me the special Jewish handshake, then." Jenny did some sort of limp wrist shake, then a high five, and then a fist bump with first the left hand and then the right hand.

Then Jenny got serious, "Do you think Irene is dead, Chipper?"

"I'm thinking she might be. I try not to think about it. I really try not to think about it. The next-door neighbors must have done her in. I feel guilty for asking her to go over there."

"Is that a tear in your eye, Chipper? I don't think I've ever seen you cry before. That is tear. I see a tear!" She wiped it away with her hand and then said, "I love you, Chipper Blair."

"It's not a tear. Not a tear." He tried to change the subject, "I forgot to tell you that Gil Hanse offered me a job. He thinks I know a lot about golf."

152

"It was a tear, wasn't it? I saw a tear. Didn't you think a job offer from Gil Hanse was a big enough deal to tell me last night? That's a very big deal. I would think you would jump at the chance. I don't want to move, though. That's a given."

"It would be part-time, only when he needs me on different courses. I could keep my driving range job. We won't be moving. He'll be at the party tonight. Make sure you find him and his team and introduce yourself. Very nice guy. Tell him we talked about it, and I said yes."

Jenny commented, "Lot of pressure on me tonight. Gil, Max, Rory, Kira K. I wish you were going. Please try to be home by three thirty, Chipper."

"Me, too. I wish I was going. I'll be home by three thirty. I love to watch you try on things. Let's go hit a few golf shots and get this day started."

Chipper then went in the bathroom and cried for Irene.

SPECIAL AGENT TRIPP

When Judith Hitten arrived at her law offices in downtown Monterey on Tuesday morning she found Special Agent Tripp waiting at the back door. For some reason, he knew she parked in the back and entered from the back door. She wasn't surprised that he knew, or that he was there. Tripp was alone and had a manila envelope in his hand.

She casually said, "Good morning. Do you want a cup of coffee?"

He said, "Yes, please. Thank you very much. I have a big day today. Seeing you this morning early, then trying to examine the Whitebread house again, then we've got some men, thanks to your friend Stein, committed to hanging out around the Clambake party at the Lodge this evening."

"Big day," was all she said as she opened the back door. She walked down the hall, with Tripp trailing behind, and started a pot of coffee. They exchanged small talk uncomfortably waiting for the coffee. When it was done, Hitten said, "Cream and sugar?"

Tripp said, "Just black."

"I would have guessed that. You know, you look like an FBI guy."

"I try."

They walked into Judith Hitten's office, and Tripp closed the door behind them. He said, "I have here a superior court judge's order to open Irene McVay's will."

"Which Judge?"

"Does it matter?"

"Just curious."

"Judge Butler."

"Good for you. She's a friend of mine. Very good judge. My favorite, but don't tell anyone that."

"I promise I won't."

"Do you want me to just tell you what's in the will, or do you have to see it?"

"I actually need a copy. Judge Butler has agreed to that, as well. Murder investigation, you know."

Hitten left her office and came back with a copy of the will. It was only a few pages long. She handed it to Tripp.

Tripp smiled broadly as he read the will. He said, "I assume the Ben and Aileen Morris trust is administered by Chipper Blair and Jenny Nelson?"

"Actually, it's administered by our office. It's a foundation that we set up for Chipper when he inherited Ben Morris' estate. His wife Jenny is the CEO of the foundation. They give away money each year based on grants from golf-related activities. It is very generous of them to do this."

Tripp just said, "So the two hundred and fifty million dollars in the will actually goes to this foundation that is basically Chipper Blair's money, right?"

"Well, legally, it really isn't his."

"But the money is controlled by Blair and his wife!"

"Technically, it is controlled by the Board of Directors. I am on the Board."

"And I assume the others on the Board are all friends of the couple?"

"Yes. It makes sense that Irene would do this. She was on the Board. She has no heirs."

"Blair knew this, obviously?"

"Chipper didn't know what was in the will. He did know Irene didn't have heirs. Chipper did not have anything to do with Irene being missing. You are barking up the wrong tree, Mr. Tripp."

"It's nice of you to defend your friend, Ms. Hitten. I have been in this business a long time. I have seen all types. Blair is obviously a serial criminal. Greed beyond any limits. Pure greed. First Morris, and now McVay. He endears himself to rich people with no heirs, then finds a way to do away with them."

"You don't know Chipper, Mr. Tripp. He just cares about golf. He doesn't care about money."

"He has you fooled, too, Ms. Hitten. Now I have one more thing to do on my list today. Arrest Blair for the murder of Irene McVay."

"How do you know she isn't just missing? How do you know she has been murdered?"

"I would bet he'll confess and tell us where the body is. We have our ways. We definitely have our ways of getting information from people."

KHASHOGGI TIME

Irene McVay was delirious, starving, and her head still throbbed with pain. She woke and found herself still sitting on the floor with her back to the wall, just to the right of the door of the wine cellar. She was freezing and shaking. She reached for her last bite of pita bread, lying on the floor in front of her. She tried to toss the plastic wrapper to the side, but it just slid back down onto the floor next to her. For some reason she started laughing uncontrollably at her plight.

When she finished the small piece of pita bread, not knowing when she might eat again, she started singing some lines from Jimmy Buffet's Margaritaville song. She couldn't figure out if she was singing out loud or just to herself. It just seemed to come into her head. She didn't remember all of the words and made up some as well.

"Nibblin' on pita cakes
Oh, how my head aches

Strummin' my six-string
Hear my front door bell ring

Wastin' away again in Margaritaville
Searchin' for my lost shaker of salt

Some people claim that there's an Arab to blame
But I know, it's my own fault"

She paused a bit, then looked at her bruised side, now very black and blue, and then continued singing again. This time she realized she was louder and the song wasn't just in her mind.

"Don't know the reason
Stayed here all season
Nothin' to show but this brand-new tattoo
But it's a real beauty
A Mexican cutie
How it got here, I GOT KICKED OVER AND OVER

Wastin' away again in Margaritaville
Searchin' for my lost shaker of salt
Some people claim that there's an Arab to blame
Now I think, hell, it could be my fault

But there's booze on the walls
God, I've had a lot
Of wine that helps me hang on"

Irene looked down to her right and saw the two bottles of Dom Perignon sitting upright. It took a while for her to realize what they were there for. "I have a plan," she said to herself. Then she yelled "I have a plan!" again. Her voice echoed against the far wall of wine racks.

After what seemed like a long time to Irene McVay, she finally heard some noises outside the door. The first sounds in what she felt was two days. The voices sounded like Arabic. Next she heard a sound she didn't like at all. Her blood froze. It sounded like a motor of some kind running.

Then the motor turned off, and she heard a man say in English, "Chainsaw works. Motor works. Khashoggi time."

Irene heard another voice say excitedly in English, "Let's get this over with. I don't know why Hassan took so long to decide to do this."

As the door knob turned and unlocked, she stood quickly and flipped the light switch off. She picked up the Dom bottles, one in each hand, and stood to the side of the door to the wine room. Her eyes were having trouble adjusting to the darkness but when the door opened and the light came from outside the room the first thing she saw appear in the doorway was the chainsaw. It was off. For now.

Irene's adrenaline and panic gave her some needed energy. Before she saw the man holding the chainsaw, she took her right hand and, holding the top of the bottle, swung the Dom Perignon bottle as hard as she could to where she guessed the head of the man entering would be. She was surprised when she felt she made direct contact with his forehead. The noise was loud and she felt another adrenaline rush. She was in survival mode.

The chainsaw fell to the ground and was quickly followed to the ground by the dark man who was holding the weapon. She retreated, with the other bottle of Dom still in her hand, to the rear of the wine room. Her back was to the wine racks. As she was retreating, she heard the other man yell, "Ali!" very loudly. The man bent over the one on the ground that he called Ali, and very efficiently put one foot on the back of the chainsaw, released the safety handle, and pulled the cord to make it start. The noise in the wine room was deafening.

The man advanced toward Irene. She put her bottle of Dom down and reached behind her and started pulling wine bottles out of the rack with both hands. She threw the bottle with her right hand, and replaced it with the bottle on her right. She was able to throw three or four and, although she hit the man, he continued to advance. There were several broken wine bottles on the floor between them. Unlike the thicker Dom bottle, they broke easily.

When the man was within a few feet of Irene he yelled "Allahu Akbar!" at the top of his lungs and lunged at her with the chainsaw. She felt the blade very close to her right arm. The man slipped on the wet floor, and the chainsaw fell and jumped forward and to the left. Irene quickly bent down and grabbed a broken wine bottle and stabbed toward the man's neck. She felt the bottle go into his neck deeply, and he again said, "Allahu Akbar" in a much softer and gurgling voice. He lay on the ground with what she felt was a good flow of blood coming from his neck.

Irene then hit him on the head with the Dom Perignon bottle. It didn't break but made quite a thud against the man's skull. She grabbed the wine bottle and stabbed him again in the neck. She yelled "Allahu Akbar!"

Then she walked slowly over to the other man, who was still out cold near the entrance of the wine room. The Dom bottle was still intact, and she struck him in anger in the head several times until the bottle finally broke. Then she retrieved the broken wine bottle and left it embedded in his neck. She was covered in blood, both her arms and her clothes.

She didn't have time to catch her breath and hoped that her intruders and possible murderers were not followed by others. She peeked out the door of the wine room and saw no one. She was going to try to scamper out but decided to go back in the room and grab another bottle of Dom Perignon and another broken red wine bottle with a very jagged edge.

She was afraid to move very quickly, as she entered the hallway toward a small flight of stairs she knew led to the next floor and would lead her close to the back door of the estate. Her energy level was dropping. She was tired. She was crying. She tried singing to herself again, *Wastin' away again in Margaritaville.* She opened the door at the top of the steps extremely slowly. She heard no voices. *Was it possible no one was in the house?* She tiptoed to the back door and opened it very slowly again, slipping out into the cold wet air. It was light out but appeared to be near dusk to her.

As she slinked around outside toward the back of the estate, she thought to herself *Free at Last! Free at Last! Thank God I'm free at Last! Now I just have to find the back gate.*

NO FUN

Chipper stood on the first tee at Spanish Bay under his tent. He was still cold and damp, even wearing a Spanish Bay logo parka he had "borrowed" from the pro shop. The course was empty again. He was enjoying hitting drivers down the first fairway occasionally from under the tent. He had to move the tent slightly to make sure the opening was facing where he wanted to hit his drive. He was looking forward to getting home early and grabbing some scotch and watching Jenny do a fashion show for him.

About eleven, another assistant pro named Charlie, who usually worked in the clubhouse, came down to the first tee. He had seen Chipper hitting balls and made sure he yelled "Fore!" before coming around to the front of the tent. Charlie was carrying a range bucket full of balls and a few clubs. "You can't be the only one having fun today, Chipper. Mind if I hit some balls with you?"

"No problem, Charlie." Chipper was unusually enthusiastic. He felt ashamed of himself for feeling that way.

Charlie's bucket of range balls were the usual red-striped "seconds," rather than the new Titleists Chipper was hitting. He said, "How can you afford to hit new balls out there and not get them back? We charge six bucks per ball in the clubhouse."

Chipper got back to his usual defensive self and said, "You know my story, Charlie. Money doesn't mean much to me now."

They decided to each hit the range balls and alternated. Their competition involved a shared agreement on who hit the shot better. They had to declare their target before hitting and say whether the shot would be a low hook, high hook, low fade, or high fade. After ten shots each, Chipper was up six to four.

Charlie suddenly blurted out, "Don't you think they took the fun out of this tournament this year? Whoever is in charge decided that, because of the amount of money the pros are playing for, the celebrity amateurs like Bill Murray and Ray Romano and Larry the Cable Guy couldn't play. Too much levity and fooling around. There are still some sports guys who can hit the ball, but they have eliminated a lot of former players."

Chipper, of course, said, "It was a ship of fools before. I hate guys who don't show the game the respect it deserves. It's fun in itself without Bill Murray dragging women into sand traps and trying to be funny. Just doing anything he feels like that makes him think he did something funny. Good riddance."

Charlie was surprised at Chipper's reaction. "You don't think the celebrities add to the fun and excitement of the tournament?"

"It's always bothered me that the majority of spectators follow the funny guys and celebrities. They wouldn't know Rory McElroy from Adam Scott. Wouldn't know Collin Morikawa from Max Homa. Crazy. Golf should be golf. Galleries should be here to watch the golfers."

"I guess I kind of agree with you, Chipper, but they have even taken away tickets for the practice rounds and eliminated the Celebrity Challenge tomorrow. No fun. At least they will still be at the Clambake tonight to provide some laughs. I assume I'll see you there?"

Chipper said, "You assume wrong. The CEO basically told my wife to keep me away, and I was not invited. I won't be there, and I really don't mind at all. I think the spectators got lucky yesterday and today. No one would walk around in this weather and watch anyway. I have a hunch not too many guys are playing practice rounds, either. This course is empty, and I bet Pebble and Spyglass are, too."

They continued to hit balls, and after another ten each, Chipper was up twelve to eight.

Chipper said, "Let's take the rest of these over to the practice green and hit some short shots."

Charlie responded, "Too wet, and I've heard about your short game."

Chipper was happy to say, "They don't call me Chipper for nothing."

Charlie took the rest of the bucket and started running toward the pro shop. Chipper thought he heard him say, "That was fun," as he was running away to get out of the rain.

Chipper sat under his tent until two PM, then decided to call it a day. He waved to the pro shop and got the thumbs up from his boss at Spanish Bay. He walked to his car and drove home.

At two forty-five, Agent Tripp and his two men walked into the pro shop and asked the head pro where Chipper was. They were told he went home early. Tripp waved an arrest warrant for Chipper in front of the head pro but didn't say what it was. Tripp was obviously disappointed and in some distress. He said to his men, "We'll get him tomorrow. We have to be at the Lodge to ensure security for the Clambake party."

THE ESCALADE CARAVAN

If anyone was driving on Highway 1 or Fremont Boulevard in Seaside, they would have been surprised to see a caravan of twelve Cadillac Escalades in a row heading to the private plane terminal at the Monterey Airport. Hassan Ahmad sat in the passenger seat of the first car in the caravan and was feeling smug. Everything was falling into place, and by the time everyone knew of the horror at Spanish Bay, he and his crew would be halfway back to Saudi Arabia. He had only lost a few expendables.

The cost of the entire operation: the houses, the cars, and the chemicals was well worth it. LIV would be the only game in town now. He was glad Irene McVay was Khashoggied, finally. He was a little surprised he hadn't heard from the last two men in the Hastings estate already but assumed all had gone well. He'd talk to them when they got to the airport.

He reached into his pocket and pulled out Amir's cell phone. He checked the time and confirmed with the two passengers in the back seat that it was four PM. When they agreed, he pulled up the app that said PBL and pressed the activation link.

Ahmad then said in Arabic, "Allahu Akbar," and smiled. The men in the back seat and the driver all responded, "Allahu Akbar!" in unison.

CHANGE OF PLANS

At four PM, The Pebble Beach Company food service crew had spent most of the day setting up tables, chairs, linens, flowers, place settings, the entertainment stage, instruments, table numbers, and cards indicating where everyone was to sit. The kitchen staff had prepped for a few days and was preparing the meal for the Clambake in the ballroom at the Lodge.

The security team had set up the metal detectors at each entrance door. Armed uniformed guards were already in place in the room and at the entrances. Security cameras were set up in several locations in the large room and monitors were testing them from the room next door so they could watch all areas of the operation that night.

Each attendee was texted a QR code that had to be scanned in order to be let in the room. Almost a year of planning had gone into the security for this event. Discussed, argued, rediscussed, and finalized.

The marketing group was responsible for hanging photos of past tournaments on the walls and had prepared a video that would show continuously on the large screens in each corner of the room during dinner.

The finishing touches were being completed, with about fifty people from the Pebble Beach Company staff in the room, when the overhead fire sprinklers spontaneously and simultaneously started spewing water all over the room. It was a deluge. It was a disaster within a few minutes. Several managers ran into the adjoining kitchen to see if anyone had started a fire or created too much smoke. No one could smell smoke.

Another manager grabbed a chair and stood on it and tried to reach one of the sprinkler heads, but he couldn't reach it. He was soaked in seconds.

Security Chief Patrick Black ran down the hall to the Corporate Offices and barged in the office of CEO Stevens. All he said was, "Disaster. Come with me." They both took off running back toward the ballroom.

Stevens, although out of breath, kept yelling, Tell me what happened," over and over again. "What the fuck happened?" Richard Stein and COO Catherine McDougall heard them yelling as the men ran by their offices, and they quickly followed down the hall. Black was out of breath, as well, and never could explain what happened. They all expected the worst.

When Stevens went through the doors to the ballroom, he gasped and immediately said, "Who the fuck is responsible for this? How could this happen?" Water was still sprinkling down from all the spigots in the ceiling. "Has anyone called Jose?" Jose Morales was the head of maintenance. "We have to turn the water to the room off. Hasn't anyone called Jose? Someone has to know how to turn the water off. What the fuck?"

But they all knew it was too late. The setup for the Clambake party was ruined, and the room itself had already sustained serious water damage. No one could reach Jose Morales. While the water was still coming down, Stevens, McDougall, Stein, and Black went out in the hall, and Stevens paused for a minute before saying, "We'll have to deal with the ballroom damage later, but for now we have to figure out what to do about the Clambake party. It's a big deal for all our sponsors, pros, and amateurs."

Without hesitation, McDougall said, "We have to cancel it, Donald. The room is unusable. What a disaster."

Stevens said, "I still want to have the party."

She said, "We don't have a big enough space left in the Lodge. Only outside, maybe." They all looked outside at the drizzle and mist and just shook their heads in disbelief.

Stevens said, just as Hassan Ahmad had planned, "The only possible alternative is the Grand Ballroom at Spanish Bay."

Stein and McDougall, almost in unison, said, "There isn't time to do that. How can we possibly set up everything over there, have food ready, music ready, and notify everyone? It's only a few hours until party time."

"We can do this. We'll do an all-hands-on-deck alert and have everyone who can, show up and help at the Inn. We can do this! We can fucking do this!"

Stein and McDougall shook their heads in disbelief. Stein said, "How can we possibly do this, Donald? Who knows who will show up from the staff?"

"We'll let anyone on the staff who comes and helps stay and watch the entertainment and see all the pros. We'll set up chairs in the other part of the Grand Ballroom and let them stay. How hard could it be to just set up the stage and the tables? Shouldn't take very long. We've got everything we need over there; tables, chairs, the stage, tablecloths, linens…"

McDougall interrupted, "The food is going to be an issue, too. The kitchen staff has to take everything that they have prepared here over to Spanish Bay."

Black was standing there and hadn't said anything. He was hoping this idea would fizzle out and he wouldn't have to step in. When he realized Stevens was going to try to do this, he finally said, "This won't work at all, Donald. We have no security set up for the Grand Ballroom at Spanish Bay. We have nothing. No cameras. No metal detectors. We haven't examined the room at all...It just can't happen in time."

Stevens was getting impatient. "What are the chances anything can really happen at this party? No one even knows we're going to have it there. All the guests are hand-selected. I have to send out my emails and texts to everyone in the staff and all the guests. Maybe we'll move it back to six thirty instead of six. If people come here, we'll bus them over. Lots to do. Lots to do. We can do this." Stevens started trotting toward his office with Stein, McDougall, and Black close behind.

Black called Special Agent Tripp while he was walking and told Tripp to come to Donald Stevens' office. In the office, Stevens was writing on a yellow pad everything that had to be done and putting either his own, Stein's, McDougall's, or Black's name next to it. That task became that person's responsibility immediately. When he was almost done with the list, Tripp, Chan, and Lopez came into the office.

Black explained what was happening, and Tripp immediately walked over to Stevens and said, "You cannot do this, Stevens. We don't have time to do proper security over there. Everything is planned for here. We have nothing there at all."

Stevens, without looking up, said, "Well, I suggest you get stuff over there! How hard is it to get the guards over there? Pretty easy, I would think. We're doing this. You have to adjust, Tripp. Can you do that?"

Tripp was almost yelling, "The FBI protests. We'll protest formally. I am advising against this most strongly. Mr. Stevens. Most strongly!"

"I can see that, Mr. Tripp. Go ahead and protest, but this is happening. This is a big deal to us. You better get moving. Mr. Tripp, and you, Mr. Black. Get out of my office and make this happen."

CHIPPER AND JENNY

Chipper arrived home about three forty-five, and Jenny and Angus were waiting impatiently. "I got here as fast as I could, Jenny. There is more traffic than usual. And the PETA people are still protesting outside our house. What the hell. Why are they still out there?"

"Because they think you're a dog killer, Chipper. Thanks for coming home earlier than usual. I was hoping you'd be here about fifteen minutes ago. I have a lot to try on."

Chipper petted Angus and said, "Do you think I'm a dog killer, Angus?" Angus rolled over on his back and enjoyed the belly rub, and Chipper said, "See, Angus doesn't think I'm a dog killer. He still loves me. Maybe I'll go outside with Angus and let them see how much he loves me. I can explain I paid a million bucks to make the charge go away."

"I don't think that's a good idea, Chipper. Maybe they'll go away if you donate a million dollars to PETA?"

"No chance. We'll just let them get wet out there as long as they want."

"Let's go upstairs and I'll start my fashion show then." As soon as Jenny said upstairs, Angus rolled over and darted away. Chipper went and got a bottle of Scotch from the Scotch closet and a glass and headed upstairs. He found Angus sitting upright on the bed. Jenny was naked already.

"I like that outfit, Jen, but I don't want you going to the party like that."

"Very funny, Mr. Chips. I guess I'm taking this too seriously. Stevens said I should look professional, even though most people dress down for this. Lot of cowboy outfits, I've been told."

Chipper poured a half glass of Scotch. No water. No ice. He sat on the side of the bed, and Angus cuddled up. "It's not bed time, Angus. We're just helping Jenny." She was taking a long time in her large walk-in closet. Hers was full of clothes. Chipper's walk-in hardly had anything in it except golf shirts. Angus was starting to doze.

Jenny came into the bedroom wearing what looked to Chipper like a business suit: a navy blazer with matching slacks. She had on a plain white blouse underneath and high heel black shoes. "You look nice," he said, "Are you going to work in a bank?" Then he added, "Is it silk?" He learned that comment from Irene McVay. It was almost always a compliment.

"No silly. It is NOT silk. It's almost tweed. I think it's too heavy. And you obviously are not impressed." Then she walked back out of the room.

When she was in the closet, her phone started dinging with messages, and Chipper said, "Should I pick it up?"

Jenny came running out, completely naked again, read her two messages, then started reading them aloud to Chipper. She had a surprised look.

"They are both from Donald Stevens," she said, "First one is to attendees of the Clambake Party." *Dear honored guests. Due to circumstances beyond our control, our famous Clambake Party has been moved to the Grand Ballroom at the Inn at Spanish Bay. The time has been moved to six thirty, but if you are there early, the bars will be open. To make it easier for you to get there, there will be buses leaving every fifteen minutes from in front of the Lodge starting at five thirty. Be assured you will have a great time, and we are looking forward to seeing you.*

Then Jenny said, "Wow. That's a change. I wonder what caused that? Maybe they needed a bigger room? Maybe they invited more people? Now I have more time to decide on what to wear, anyway."

"The second one is to all Pebble Beach staff. I guess I am one." She read, *To all our great Pebble Beach staff: All hands on deck. We have been forced to move the Clambake party, unexpectedly, from the ballroom at the Lodge to the Grand Ballroom at the Inn at Spanish Bay. We need help in setting up the room and are in a rush to do this. No matter what your job, please come and help us at the Grand Ballroom. Make sure you bring your employee I.D. In honor of your help, you can stay in the room for the entertainment and seeing the celebrities, the amateurs, and the best golfers in the world. Please come and help as soon as you can.*

All Chipper felt like saying was "You have a great body. I didn't hear a word you said. I wonder if I got the same message. My phone is downstairs." He poured himself another half glass of Scotch. Angus was sound asleep, snoring loudly now. Soon Chipper might be sound asleep, snoring loudly as well.

Jenny left the room and came back a few minutes later wearing a long blue formal dress, with a slit up the side all the way to mid-thigh. "Too formal?" she said.

Chipper smiled and said, "I think that's the dress you were wearing at the Hastings dinner party the first time I saw you dressed up. I agree, too formal, and I don't want anyone staring at your leg."

"Nice try, Chipper. It's similar but not the same dress."

"Silk?" he asked again.

"Now you are just fumbling. No, it's not silk." She left the room again.

When she came back she was wearing a little black dress. "I think this is the one. I should have just put this on first."

"It's a little short, isn't it?" Chipper commented.

"I'll make sure not to bend down too much. Do you like it?"

"Of course I like it. Just make sure you don't bend over, please."

"Is Chipper jealous? I love only you, Chipper. Well, maybe I'll bend over a bit, so Max Homa sees me."

She then tried on a set of pearls and a pearl bracelet, looked in the full length mirror, and nodded in approval at the way she looked. "I think I'll go a bit early and see if I can help out with whatever they need done. Maybe Kira will be there early. I'm sorry you aren't going, Chipper. Why don't you just go anyway? There will be a lot of people there."

"It's not my kind of deal, you know that. Make sure you introduce yourself to Gil Hanse and tell him who you are. I like him. Have fun. Take some photos. I'll just be here drinking."

Jenny gave Chipper a kiss on the forehead and headed downstairs. Angus didn't budge.

IRENE

Irene McVay moved as fast as she could past the guest house and into the back area of what was now Richard Stein's estate. When Irene was staying in the house to comfort Emily Hastings after the death of her husband and son, she and Emily and Serena Antonelli, who was living in the guest house, used to go out walking and running early in the morning. Irene was familiar with the back of the estate and knew there was a gate behind some bushes that lead to a path where she could get to Pebble Beach Golf Course. She still had a full bottle of Dom Perignon in one hand and a broken bottle of some sort of red wine in the other.

The terrain was muddy and rocky and she was still very confused. She was muttering to herself and finally dropped the red wine bottle in the mud. It seemed there was no one following her. She could tell it was getting near dusk, and she was carefully making her way out the gate and to the path. She had no plan but just wanted to get to the golf course and find her way to her own house.

The path led between two fences that bordered other estates. She knelt down and rested for a few minutes. She could barely get up to walk. When she thought she heard the sound of footsteps behind her, she tried to jog but immediately fell to her knees into the dirt. She scraped her arm on the fence to her right. Irene waited for several minutes, her hand cocked and ready to swing the bottle of Dom, if needed, but no one came. She started sobbing uncontrollably and put her dirty hand over her mouth to muffle the sound.

She knew the 17-Mile Drive was ahead, and when she reached it, she looked both ways to make sure no cars were coming and then hobbled across the road. She knew the golf course wasn't far away. It was beginning to get dark.

Casey Boyns and Kevin Price, two Pebble Beach caddies, were on the thirteenth tee at Pebble Beach, hurrying to tee off in order to finish before dark. Boyns was one under par and Price was six over. Boyns, now in his late sixties, is in the California Golf Hall of Fame as a multiple winner of both California Amateur and Senior Amateur events. He still had a scratch handicap and is the oldest caddie at Pebble Beach Golf Course. Price was a friend of Boyns. They knew this was the last time during tournament week they would be able to play the golf course. They both had carts, so they wouldn't have to waste time going from Boyns' ball, usually down the middle, to Price's ball, usually much shorter and down the right side of every fairway.

They hit quickly off the thirteenth tee and both jumped in their carts and sped toward their golf balls. Price, on the right as usual, was the first to see the ragged woman, holding a bottle of champagne, come staggering toward the fairway. He wanted to ignore her, but she approached his cart as he was reaching his ball. He kept the cart between him and the obviously crazed and delusional woman. She was muttering something about Margaritaville.

Price could see she was in distress and said, "Are you alright, ma'am?" still keeping the cart between himself and the woman. She was strangely dressed in a tennis outfit, mud all over, blood on her arms. Her hair was a tangled mess. She didn't answer him, and he was anxious to hit his golf ball. Boyns was waiting in the middle of the fairway and couldn't tell what was going on.

Boyns yelled, "Hit the ball already, Kevin!"

Price asked her again, "Can I help you in any way, ma'am?"

All Irene McVay could say was, "Take me to my house."

"Where is your house?" he asked.

"Near the eleventh fairway."

He said quickly, "No can do. That's the other direction. We have to finish the round. Casey is one under. I'm six over."

"I need help," she said, "Wasting away in Margaritaville."

"I can't go backward, ma'am. Very sorry."

Irene, without asking, got in the passenger side of the golf cart. Price didn't know what to do, so he hit his shot and then drove toward the green. Irene could barely sit upright. Price was afraid. She still had the champagne bottle in her hand. She was a mess.

When Boyns drove alongside, he said, "What's up with her, Kevin?"

"I have no idea. She seems drunk and very weird. I can't push her out of the cart and just leave her here. I'll just let her ride in and then see what can be done with her when we are finished."

Price got out of the cart to chip near the green and said, "Can I call someone for you?" Irene McVay didn't answer. She was just slumped down in the seat staring straight ahead. Price made bogey, and Boyns made par, and they drove to the fourteenth tee.

Both hit decent drives and, when they reached the middle of the fourteenth fairway, left their carts to hit their second shots. Price yelled, as Irene McVay left the cart and started wandering off toward the right of the fairway, "Where are you going?"

She fell a few times but kept getting up and heading toward Chipper's back yard.

Boyns and Price just looked at each other. Boyns said, "Very strange."

Price said, "It looks like she knows where she is going anyway. Crazy lady."

Boyns said, "You're away, Kevin."

THE CLAMBAKE PARTY

Jenny drove to the Inn at Spanish Bay and was behind several cars waiting to valet park near the entrance. She counted that she was fifth in line. When she got to the front, the young driving attendant came around and politely helped her open the driver's door. She was careful getting out, but the young man was noticeably staring at her legs when she exited. He smiled at her as he gave her a ticket stub.

When she entered the Inn and made the right turn past the desk to go toward the Grand Ballroom, she was greeted by two security guards who asked her to show the QR code on her phone before letting her pass. Another guard about five feet later told her to stop, and he waved a wand of some kind up and down her front side, then had her turn around, and did the same thing on her back side. He gave her the same smile as the car valet but this time said, "Good to go, ma'am."

She then walked, unimpeded, to the elevator and up to the Grand Hallway outside the Grand Ballroom. There she was met by another security guard who told her to put her cell phone in a plastic bag and write her name in the space provided. She told the guard she needed her phone. The guard said, "No one gets in without giving up their phone. No pictures. No interruptions. Absolutely no social media. Turn in your phone, or you won't get in."

The hallway was like a beehive, with people walking everywhere, carrying chairs, metal trays with food, boxes, musical instruments, tablecloths. Jenny entered the ballroom, again unimpeded, and saw what she guessed was seventy-five people doing various things. Some hanging pictures on the walls, some setting up tables, some moving bars and alcohol into place, many just standing around doing nothing. Many heads turned her way when she walked in. She heard a few wolf whistles.

Jenny recognized a few people and finally saw Richard Stein and his girlfriend Debbie standing in a corner near where a bar was being set up. Both already had a cocktail in their hands. Richard gave Jenny a big hug and said, "You look nice. Do you want a drink?" She saw Big Bill O'Shea, with the help of one other man, carrying large round tables across the room and setting them up.

"I thought I would come over early and help, if I could." Someone standing nearby heard her and asked Jenny and Debbie to start putting place settings and glasses on the tables that were already set up, and had tablecloths in place. Debbie held on to her drink and followed Jenny toward several boxes with utensils. Debbie half-heartedly grabbed a few with her free hand, while Jenny enthusiastically hurried to set tables.

Debbie said, "You do look nice, Jenny. Where is Chipper?"

"Chipper is persona non grata here. Donald Stevens doesn't like him. I wish he was here. He's home getting drunk on Scotch right now."

"I think I would rather be home drinking than here. Richard is in his glory. Look at him with the cowboy clothes. I'm surprised he didn't wear chaps over his Levi's."

Jenny asked, "What happened that caused the party to move?"

"Richard just told me they had a malfunction of the sprinkler system in the other ballroom. Everything was set up, and it was ruined. I'm surprised they didn't cancel this."

"Me, too," said Jenny, quickly.

As Jenny continued putting out place settings, she recognized several pro golfers coming into the room, with most heading to the bar. She recognized Shane Lowry, Matt Fitzpatrick, Wyndham Clark, Tommy Fleetwood, and Justin Rose. It seemed the English golfers grouped together, each with a beer, rather than a mixed drink. Patrick Cantlay and Xander Schauffele walked in together, and each looked like they had a mixed drink of some kind. Jordan Speith, Rickie Fowler, and Justin Thomas walked in together and headed for the bar.

Jenny thought to herself, *I should go over there and talk to those guys. Rickie is really cute. Shorter than I expected. I'm taller than him. Jordan is really handsome. Looks better in person than on TV.* She said to Debbie, who was still hanging around her, "Let's go and introduce ourselves to those guys over there."

Debbie said, "Who are they? The one guy dressed in orange is very cute."

"You don't know who they are? I'm surprised. Come on. Let's go."

Jenny and Debbie walked over, and Jenny got in the bar line behind Justin Thomas. She tapped him on the shoulder and said, "Mr. Thomas. I'm Jenny Nelson. I'm a teaching pro here."

Thomas didn't hide the fact he was looking at Jenny from head to toe, and he surprised her by saying, "I know you. You are the pro in the Cindy Project videos. You did a great job with her. She made the team. And to the question everyone asks, Cindy or Jenny, I definitely pick Jenny."

All she could say was, "Thank you very much, Mr. Thomas. I'm surprised you watched some of those."

"Call me Justin. I watched all of them, and if you ask any pro in here, I bet they did, too." Thomas made Rickie and Jordan turn around and asked, "You guys know who this is?"

Rickie Fowler said, "It's Jenny. My choice, as well, in the Cindy vs. Jenny debate."

Jordan Speith said, "That makes it unanimous. I'm a Jenny man, as well, but don't tell my wife about this."

Jenny was a bit embarrassed but proud to be recognized. When she got to the front of the line, she ordered a martini. Debbie did the same. They were going to stand around and relish the attention of the three golfers when Kira K. Dixon ran across the floor and hugged Jenny hard. "Shoshy. My Shoshy. Great to see you. You look incredible. How is Chipper? Where is Chipper?"

Jordan said, "Well, hello, Miss America, glad to see you again. How do you know Jenny?"

"We've known each other since I was a young teen. I love her."

Jenny said, "Chipper was told not to come by Mr. Stevens. I'm on my own."

Kira said, "We have to sit together. Let's go put some stuff on a table to reserve our spots."

Jenny followed Kira over to a table near the stage, and they picked up the table napkins and draped them over their chairs. Kira said, "It's too bad my pro from last year, Zac Blair, didn't qualify this year. I can't even play. I'm doing announcing, and the amateurs only get to play on Thursday and Friday. Next year, I'm hoping to not play, because we're going to try to have a baby. I hope to be pregnant at this time next year. How about you?"

"Chipper and I talked about it. He wants to leave it to chance. He says when one of us makes the morning shot, then we'll try to have a baby."

"That might be never," Kira commented. Jenny frowned.

As they stood and chatted, the room was filling up. Bill Murray went up to the stage unannounced and grabbed the microphone. "Welcome, all my close friends, to my Clambake party. Clambake is a very strange word. We're not going to have clams. That's awful. Does anyone even like clams? Can you all believe? I say, can you all believe? Jordan Speith, can you believe? Rickie, can you believe? That they won't even let me play this year! I can't believe it. No one can believe it. No one will buy tickets. Everyone who buys tickets wants to see me play all four rounds. Now all I can do is sit around and drink. I hope it rains and soaks all you fuckers for four days in a row." Then he stepped off the stage and headed to the bar.

Without introduction again, Darius Rucker and Clay Walker, walked up on stage with a few musicians. There was some tuning up, then they started a sing-along of Bing's classic:

Fore!

Straight down the middle
It went straight down the middle
Then it started to hook just a wee, wee bit
That's when my caddie lost sight of it
That little white pellet has never been found to this day
But it went straight down the middle like they say

Whack down the fairway
It went smack down the fairway
Then it started to slice just a smidge off line
It headed for two then it bounced off nine
My caddie says, "Long as you're still in the state, you're okay"
Yes, it went straight down the middle, quite a ways

The sun was never brighter
The greens were never greener
And I was never keener to play
I heard it came down the middle
It went zing down the middle

Oh, the life of a golfer is not all gloom
There's always the lies in the locker room
And I'm in my glory when wrapped in a towel, I say
That it went straight down the middle today

Oh, the life of a golfer is not all gloom
Though they charge you for listening in the locker room
But I'm in my glory when wrapped in a towel, I say
That it went straight down the middle
Where it wound up is a riddle
But it went straight down the middle far away

Jenny took a quick glance around the room and noticed the newest pro Nick Dunlap was seated with two other young pros, Ludvig Aberg and Cameron Young. There was a table of Asian pros, including Tom Kim, S.H. Kim, Si Woo Kim, Sungjae Im, Brandon Wu, Kevin Yu, and Ben An. She debated going by a table full of NFL quarterbacks (Tom Brady, Aaron Rodgers, Josh Allen, Alex Smith, and Steve Young) but decided not to. She thought to herself, *I really should go introduce myself to Tom Brady* but didn't. *He'll get to see me when I get my award anyway. That's good enough. Oh, there is Rory. There is Scottie. They'll get to see me get my award, too. What a great evening.*

IRENE AND CHIPPER

When Jenny left, Chipper, with Angus at his heels, took his bottle of scotch and his glass down the stairs to the study and turned on the golf channel. He immediately hit the mute button when he saw Brandel Chamblee, Paul McGinley, and Rich Lerner sitting at a table overlooking the eighteenth hole at Pebble Beach. The talking heads were at it again, talking endlessly about the golf course and the Signature Tournament that would start the day after tomorrow. Chipper didn't mind Rich Lerner, but the mute button was his safety from Chamblee and McGinley.

He poured himself his third half-glass of Scotch and wondered what Jenny was doing at the Clambake party. He wondered why she hadn't sent any photos or texted him yet about what was going on. He enjoyed the scenes on the TV of his own Pebble Beach and the rain. It was getting dark outside, but the floodlights were on, and the eighteenth green was illuminated.

Chipper pretended to comment on what Chamblee and McGinley were saying. "For those of you that don't know, I am Brandel Chamblee. I used to play on the Tour. Listen to how much knowledge I have about golf and the elusive perfect golf swing. We are looking at the hole where the tournament will be decided on Sunday. Well, maybe Monday, if we have some rain delays. It's raining hard now, as it usually does at Pebble Beach this time of the year. I'm liking Patrick Cantlay this week: knows the course, great ball striker, on top of his game. What do you think, Paul?"

Chipper stood up and paced back and forth with his glass of Scotch and tried to put on a British accent. Angus paced back and forth with him, underfoot. "My friend, Brandel, as usual you are wrong. Cantlay doesn't have a good record at Pebble Beach. My pick is Shane Lowry, unless he has too much beer at the Clambake Party. I saw him earlier today in the pub, and I think he is ready to win. In the wet and sloppy weather, I have to go with either a Brit, a Scotsman, or an Irishman."

Angus, unexpectedly, started running around the room, and looking very anxious. He started barking and quickly exited the study. Chipper yelled, "What's up, Angus? What's up, dog? Come back here."

Angus continued to bark but did come back in the room and looked up at Chipper with a puzzled look. Then he took off out of the room again and continued barking until Chipper finally followed. Chipper followed him to the back door where Angus started scratching the door and barking even more wildly. He was jumping up and down and banging against the door. Chipper said, "So, you have to go to the bathroom, you crazy mutt." Chipper then opened the door, and Angus ran out, still barking wildly.

Chipper watched as Angus headed down the stairs and then stopped and licked Irene McVay on the face. Chipper hurried down the steps and said out loud, "Irene. Irene. You're alive! You're back!"

Irene was unconscious, about halfway up the stairs to the back door. She was a complete mess: dirty, wet, blood in many places, and for some reason wearing a ripped and disheveled tennis outfit. Or what used to be a tennis outfit. Angus was till licking her face, even though it had blood and dirt all over it. Chipper's thoughts raced. He tried to wake her. He held her head in both his hands. He bent over and made sure she was breathing. He thought to himself, *Can I pick her up? I should get her to the car and take her to the emergency room at the hospital. It's close. Should I wash her first? Wrap her in a blanket? Where the hell has she been all this time? She looks awful. Should I try to give her water? Should I just call 911? That might take too long. She looks bad.* He was paralyzed and didn't know what to do.

Finally, he struggled to pick her up. He was afraid of tripping and falling down the stairs backwards. He was afraid of dropping Irene. He had a picture in his head of dropping her and Irene sliding down the stairs to the turf below. He negotiated the stairs successfully and decided to just continue to the car and get her to the emergency room. He was shaking. Tougher than first tee jitters in a golf tournament.

He managed to turn her and get her in the back seat of his car. He wasn't worried about the mess and the blood. He tried to seatbelt her body in but could only buckle one around her knees. Hopefully she won't roll over. Before Chipper could close both doors, Angus hopped in and was lying on Irene's chest, continuing to lick her face and neck. Chipper checked the time and it was five forty-five. It was dark out. He gunned his car out of the driveway and, when he was on the 17-Mile Drive, he called 911 on his phone.

The operator didn't even have time to talk when Chipper said, "I have a woman in a bad way that I am taking to the emergency room at CHOMP. Can you please have them waiting with help and a wheelchair or stretcher?"

The operator said, "I am sending them a message now as I am talking to you. I'll stay on the line, sir. What is wrong with her? Heart attack?"

"She is not breathing very well. She has been missing for about ten days and just showed up. She is in a bad way. Looks beat up and dirty. Smells bad."

"Don't panic, sir. You sound nervous. Drive carefully. How far away are you?"

"Probably six or seven minutes only. I'm hanging up. I'll be there soon. Thank you."

When the 911 operator said, "What is your name, sir? What is the woman's name, sir?" Chipper had already hung up.

He skidded to a stop underneath the hospital at the parking area near the emergency room entrance. He was overjoyed there was a team of four waiting with a gurney. They dragged Irene McVay out of the car carefully and slowly, put her on the gurney, and took her into the E.R. Angus jumped out and followed the gurney. No one could stop him.

Chipper parked his car. It was difficult to find a spot, so he parked in a yellow zone. He decided to quickly call Jenny. She didn't answer, so he left a short message that he was at the E.R. with Irene. Then he texted Jenny, Big Bill O'Shea, and Richard Stein that Irene showed up, and he was with her at the E.R. at Community Hospital of Monterey Peninsula (CHOMP). They would not see the text, because their phones were outside the Grand Ballroom.

Chipper didn't think of contacting anyone else. All he could think of was racing back inside to see how Irene was doing. Angus was being held calmly in the arms of a nurse when Chipper ran in. He yelled, "Where did she go?"

All the nurse said was, "You have to go put this dog in the car. Nice dog but not sterile."

Chipper took Angus in his arms and ran back to the car. "You've been gaining weight, Angus. Have to put you on a diet." Angus dropped down into the front seat willingly. Chipper cracked both the front windows a bit and said, "I'll be back as soon as I can, Angus." He glanced at the digital clock in the car, and it was ten after six. Then he sprinted back inside.

The same nurse was waiting for him at the entrance and said, "Sir. You have to fill out some paperwork."

"How is she doing?"

"I don't know sir. They took her away."

"Away where?"

"Please come with me and fill out some paperwork. Are you related to the patient?"

"Just a friend. I have to see Irene, please. I have to go inside."

Chipper was already out of breath, panicked, and tired. He ran away from the nurse, past the admitting desk, pushed through some double doors, and looked both ways. The two nurses were trying not to shout too loud, but both were saying, "You can't go in there, sir."

Chipper turned to the right and pushed back some curtains and saw four gowned medical people standing over Irene. She had an I.V. drip going into her arm. One of the medical people had a compress that she was using to wash Irene's face. Irene was covered by what looked like several blankets. A man with a name tag saying Dr. Hansen stood in front of Chipper and calmly said, "Are you the man who brought her in?"

"Yes."

"It's good you got her here. She was very severely dehydrated. Is she an alcoholic? I've never seen someone so dehydrated. I think when we treat that with the I.V. drips and get her out of danger, then we'll start dealing with her other issues. It looks like she has been severely beaten, as well."

"Is she going to be OK?"

"We hope so."

At this point, Irene started talking nonsense, again saying, "I'm in Margaritaville. Can't get out. Help me out." Her eyes were not focusing but were looking straight at the ceiling.

Dr. Hansen said to Chipper, "You know, don't take this personally, but in these type of cases, we call the police. You have to wait here in the waiting room for questioning. I'm sure that will be OK for you?"

Chipper said, "Her name is Irene McVay. Go ahead and call the police. We think she was kidnapped and held by a group of Arabs calling themselves the Whitebreads, who live in an estate off the fourteenth fairway at Pebble Beach."

One of the medical personnel wrote Irene's name on the chart on the nightstand. Chipper then said, "My name is Chipper Blair. I am a friend. She showed up at my back door like this."

Hansen tried to lead Chipper out of the area, but Chipper resisted and leaned over Irene. He stared in her face. She murmured, "Chipper. Is that you? I love you. Am I OK? Too many margaritas."

Hansen and one of the other people tried to pull Chipper back gently, but he insisted. "Was it the Arabs?"

Irene whispered in her weak voice, "Arabs. Khashoggi. Clambake. Chemicals. Watch out."

They all listened intently and no longer tried to rush Chipper out. Irene said again, "Saw chemicals. Clambake party. Bad news."

Hansen said, "What do you think she means by that? She's obviously delirious."

Chipper yelled, "I love you, Irene!" He immediately texted Jenny, Bill, and Richard again and simply said, "Get the fuck out of there NOW. Don't eat anything." He tried calling Jenny again with the same no answer. He told the doctors to call the police and sheriff's departments and have them send as many officers as they could over to the Inn at Spanish Bay. NOW!"

Hansen again said, "You can't trust anything she says. She's just repeating words that come into her mind. It could be from a TV show, a book, anything that she read in a newspaper."

Chipper didn't hear the last part of what the doctor said. He was out the door, running again to his car.

He also didn't hear Hansen say, "We aren't going to call the police, either. Just random words from a sick woman. Now, let's try to make her better."

CLAMBAKE DINNER

Jenny and Kira had a lot to talk about. Debbie wandered over to the bar and brought herself and Jenny two more martinis back to the table. Richard Stein, wearing a cowboy hat, followed Debbie back and put his hat down on his place setting. He was enjoying Jake Owen, who had taken the stage and was singing a few country songs. Debbie was embarrassed when Stein started doing what he thought was the Texas Two-Step. Fortunately, not many people were watching.

Jenny noticed that besides the round dinner tables, which were almost all set up now, with people claiming their spots, there were what she guessed to be seventy-five folding chairs set up on one side of the room for the Pebble Beach employees who helped do the room setup. She finished her second martini and was feeling no pain and decided to figure out which person was Gil Hanse, so she could say hello, as Chipper asked her to.

Stein pointed at the table with CEO Donald Stevens and other high executives in the Pebble Beach Corporation. PGA Commissioner Jay Monahan was seated at the same table. She started walking over but was reluctant to interrupt any conversations. Hanse, as Stein pointed out, was standing next to Stevens, but they appeared to be talking to other people nearby, rather than each other. She tapped Hanse on the shoulder and said, "I'm Jenny Nelson, my husband Chipper wanted me to make sure

I introduced myself to you." Hanse smiled, and Jenny was impressed that he looked her right in the eyes and didn't give her the once over. She thought to herself, *He showed me some class and some respect.*

When Stevens heard the name, Chipper, he turned around quickly, gave Jenny a slow look from head to toe, winked, and said, "I don't want to hear that name here tonight, even if it is your husband. This is supposed to be a fun night." Hanse looked at Jenny, showing some embarrassment at Steven's comment.

Hanse said, "So nice to meet you, Jenny. I found your husband to be quite knowledgeable about both golf and golf architecture. I've been in the business a long time, and I found his candor refreshing. He made some great comments about our renovation of the golf course here."

Stevens gave out a sigh and turned back around to continue his conversation while Jenny said, "Thank you very much, Mr. Hanse. He certainly knows his golf. Lives for golf. There is no one like Chipper."

Without turning around this time, Stevens said, "I think I just heard the name again." He thought he was being funny.

Hanse continued, "And I hear you are quite the teaching pro, getting an award tonight from Golf Digest. Great place to have it presented. Everyone who is anyone in the golf world is here tonight. What a great party. Congratulations. Has Chipper" he whispered, "said anything about my job offer?"

"He was quite pleased, actually. I think you are going to have a new employee, as long as he can keep his job here at the driving range." Jenny was whispering as well now.

There was a slight commotion, and both looked up to see Condoleezza Rice entering the room with her two bodyguards. She didn't stop to talk to anyone but waved at each person she passed, like a beauty queen, with just a raised hand and a flick of the wrist. Jenny noticed that she headed right toward the table where Jenny and Kira had saved seats. Jenny was anxious to get back to her table and thanked Gil Hanse again before walking over. Rice was standing at the table talking to Kira. Her two bodyguards had walked over to the corner nearest the table, trying to be inconspicuous.

Jenny walked up, and Kira started to introduce Jenny by saying, "Ms. Rice, this is my..."

Condoleezza immediately said, "Hi Jenny, how are you? Nice to see you again. Kira, Jenny and I had quite the experience out at Cypress Point several months ago. If I may say so, it was very wild. Shots fired. Shots fired." And she hugged Jenny and started laughing. "Jenny handled the situation quite well. I was impressed. Can I sit at your table with you girls?"

Kira said, "We would be honored. It's not our table. It's your table now."

Jake Owen gave up the microphone mid-song to Steve John, the tournament director. John tapped the microphone and asked everyone to be seated. Jenny noticed the two seats at the other side of Kira were saved, as well, and was overjoyed when Max Homa and Collin Morikawa walked over quickly and took the two seats. Kira hugged Max. Max glanced over at Jenny and whispered, "Hi, Jenny. Where is Cindy?" Jenny was incredulous. Kira whispered to Max, "She's Jewish, too."

Max walked over to Jenny and gave her a hug and said, "Do you know the secret handshake? It seems all the Jews are at this table." Then he paraphrased a line from the Adam Sandler Chanukah song, "What a fine looking bunch of Jews!" Richard Stein got up and gave Max a hug as well. Max Homa recoiled a bit and then took his seat. Jenny had an ear-to-ear smile. She held hands with Kira.

Steve John continued from the stage, "Would Donald Stevens please come up and join me, and we'll get this Clambake started." He waited while Stevens approached the stage and climbed a few steps to stand next to John. John continued, "Welcome to all our Pro competitors. You are the best in the business. And to our business associates, we thank you for your continued support. This is a special year. Our first as a signature event. We discontinued some traditions, but this Clambake dinner is one that we wanted to continue...."

Bill Murray stood up and yelled, "I want to play golf tomorrow! I still want to play golf!" There was some muted laughter.

John continued, "Maybe next year, Bill. Maybe next year. I'll make this short. I want to thank CEO Donald Stevens for hosting this event and making this dinner happen. Behind the scenes, it was chaos, but look at this beautiful room. All this happened on short notice when we had to change the venue. Donald, why don't you say a few words."

Stevens relished the opportunity to take the microphone. "As you all know we had to unexpectedly change the venue of this great Clambake dinner. If you look over to the right you'll see many on our Pebble Beach Company staff who made this happen. Can we please give them a big round of applause?" He paused for a few seconds.

Bill Murray yelled, "Let's eat, Donald! I'm hungry, and these guys have to get home early! Next year let me play! What's for dinner?"

Ray Romano, who was sitting at the same table as Murray yelled, "Yes! Let us play! We are the ones who made this tournament! It's always been about the celebrities!" Then he and Bill Murray stood and yelled, "Let us play! Let us play! Let us play!" Stevens and John were not happy.

Finally, Stevens said, "I'm glad you asked about the food, Bill. We had planned a wonderful Chicken Cordon Bleu, prepared by our executive chefs at the Lodge, but in the short time we had to prepare for dinner here at the Inn, we had to change the menu quickly. I want to thank our excellent chefs at the Inn for tonight's banquet. We have a buffet, actually, with several choices. Sorry we are not serving you. We have the famous Sticks burger. We have a veggie lasagna. We have a cauliflower pie. It's delicious. We have mixed greens. We have Sticks tater tots. And mixed vegetables. We're sure you'll like it. Just no chicken. Thanks again to the staff. Now eat up, everyone, and enjoy the entertainment."

As Stevens and John were departing the stage, Murray yelled again, "What about drinks?"

Stevens returned to the stage and said, "Mixed drinks available at the bar. Each table will be getting several bottles of wine." And on cue, several servers appeared holding many bottles of wine and started making the rounds putting them on the tables. Jenny quickly poured herself and Kira and Debbie a full glass of cabernet each. She noticed that Condoleezza drank white. Max and Collin each had a half glass of red.

Darius Rucker returned to the stage and started singing *Only Wanna Be with You,* his biggest hit.

THE SECOND CLICK

Hassan Ahmad was getting impatient at the Monterey Jet Center, across the Monterey Airport runway from the regular passenger terminal. He was expecting fourteen passengers on his private plane, and only twelve had arrived. He had called the two missing operatives, but there was no response on their phones. He had to leave in the next ten minutes. He boarded the plane and told the pilot and copilot to prepare for takeoff.

Ahmad looked at Amir's phone and confirmed it was six thirty. His first click on Amir's phone had started the deluge in the Pebble Beach Lodge ballroom. Now, with another simple click on the other app, he set in motion the final part of the plan that he had been preparing for the past year. Everything was going perfectly so far. The click started immediately raising the temperature near the chemical bags that Amir had placed in the ceiling fan vents of the Grand Ballroom at the Inn at Spanish Bay.

He pictured in his mind what would happen in the ballroom in about forty-five minutes. The chemicals would release, the room would be filled with the mix of deadly chemicals, everyone would doze off, and fifteen minutes after that, LIV would be the only golf tour.

Ahmad sat down next to the man they called the Chemist, and they conversed in Arabic as the plane rolled down the runway and ascended into the sky. The plane would fly about fourteen hours to Mohammed V airport in Casablanca, then on to Riyadh a few days later. Ahmad was looking forward to two days in Casablanca for some relaxation. He expected to be appropriately rewarded by the Crown Prince when arriving in Saudi Arabia, adding to his already vast wealth.

The Chemist assured Hassan Ahmad that the blame would be placed on the Pebble Beach Corporation for some sort of Legionnaires' disease or carbon monoxide poisoning causing the deaths. He assured Ahmad that no one could determine the cause of death from the concoction of chemicals he had created. The Chemist knew he was lying, but it didn't matter to him. He had done his job, and he was still alive to talk about it. He was planning on disappearing when the plane arrived in Casablanca. He had already arranged his itinerary and escape.

The Chemist asked, "Won't it seem suspicious that all of you flew out and abandoned the estate you paid so much money for? Seems very suspicious to me."

"Even if there is no evidence to link us to the deaths, we would be questioned forever. I didn't want to go through the hassle. Just a hassle."

"What about the millions you paid for the estate?"

"Money doesn't really matter, does it? What is seventy-five million in cash, really? Now we'll control the golf world. Lots of money to be made. It's a good investment. We'll let the realtors and the Pebble Beach Corporation figure out what to do with the abandoned property."

"Why didn't you just set off a bomb in the room? Sure thing, right?"

"You ask too many questions. Too difficult to smuggle a bomb in there. Also, then everyone knows it's a terrorist attack, as they refer to it. With your work, we are safe. Don't ask so many questions."

Hassan Ahmad indicated to the Chemist he didn't want to talk anymore. He fell asleep, confident all would work out as planned.

CHIPPER IS DESPERATE

Chipper Blair ran to his car and found Angus sitting patiently behind the wheel. He pushed Angus aside, started the car, spun the wheels and took off out of the parking lot. There was a car in front of him going very slowly, so he honked his horn loudly and started yelling for the driver to get out of his way. His screams were contained to his own car, and the car in front was going too slowly. Chipper swerved to go around him into the entrance lane, rather than the exit lane and drove on the wrong side of the road until he turned right on Holman Highway, Highway 68 toward Pacific Grove. It was a windy two-lane road with a lot of traffic. It was tournament week.

It should only take ten minutes to get to the Inn on a regular day. He hoped he was on time. Angus was thrown back in the seat and crawled on the floor to be safer. Chipper called the main number of the Inn at Spanish Bay and, before the operator had time to ask him what he wanted, he shouted, "Tell everyone in the ballroom to get out immediately. Get out now!"

He was halfway paying attention to the dangerous road in front of him and trying to concentrate on his phone call. "Tell them to get out of the ballroom!"

The operator excitedly said, "Who is this? Why would I do that?"

Chipper yelled back, "Just get security to get everyone out! I expect an attack of some kind. In fact, it may already be happening."

"No, sir. It's pretty calm here. I don't hear any commotion."

"Let me talk to security, then!"

"As I understand it, everyone in security is at the ballroom now. It's got to be safe, sir."

"Call security anyway and let me talk to them." He waited about thirty seconds until the operator came back on and said, "No one is answering, sir." Chipper hung up.

Chipper had made a few unsafe passes on Highway 68 and had reached his left turn at Sunset Drive. The speed limit was twenty-five miles per hour, and he knew from experience it was well patrolled by Pacific Grove police waiting to give tickets. He was driving fifty past Pacific Grove High School and knew he wouldn't stop even if the police were behind him. In fact, it would be better if they were.

He took the left turn at 17-Mile Drive in Pacific Grove without stopping at the stop sign. Other motorists were honking as he almost hit a car coming across the intersection. As he sped through the pines on both sides of the road, he knew that the guard gate would require a slowdown. He knew the Pebble Beach resident sticker on his car would get him in without stopping. He barely slowed as he went through the resident lane, still going very fast. He saw the gate guard give the slowdown signal with his hands. It didn't matter. He was now desperate.

He didn't have much farther to go until the Spanish Bay signs told him to turn right. He had a quick thought to himself, *What if I am wrong about this? This could be bad. But what if I am right? I have to do this.*

Chipper skidded to a stop in the traffic circle and pulled up on the sidewalk near the front door to the Inn at Spanish Bay. He quickly opened his door and yelled, "Keys are in the ignition!" to the two valet guys running toward his car. Angus barely had time to get out the front door before it slammed behind Chipper. The valets continued yelling at him as he entered the Inn and encountered the first two security guards at the door. Luckily, they were not expecting anyone to come to the Clambake party so late and were not prepared as he rushed in and right past them. Angus was right behind him. Chipper had completely forgotten Angus was with him and didn't realize the dog was following him.

Chipper knew he had to turn right past the check-in desk and head for the stairs. He didn't want to wait for the elevator. The two security guards hesitated, then started running after him.

He bounded up the stairs to the Grand Ballroom floor, taking a few steps at a time. He tripped once to his knees, quickly got up, and continued. When Chipper fell, Angus passed him. Chipper yelled, "Oh shit, Angus!" but it was too late to do anything about the dog. He reached the Hall of the Grand Ballroom and was surprised to see Special Agents Tripp, Chan, and Lopez standing near the first door to the ballroom. The door was open, and they were looking into the room listening to Darius Rucker singing. Their backs were toward Chipper.

Chipper didn't have time to think and reacted instinctively by running right past the FBI agents and into the room screaming at the top of his lungs. Angus followed.

CHAOS AT THE CLAMBAKE

The head table of Pebble Beach executives were the first to the buffet line and were filling their plates when Chipper Blair rushed into the room yelling, "Get out! Everyone get out of this room. Get the fuck out of the room!"

Jenny immediately recognized Chipper's voice, and her emotions ran between alarm and embarrassment. She was the first one to stand up, quickly followed by about half the crowd. Stevens, at the buffet table, was livid, and before he recognized Chipper, he was looking around the room trying to see what security was doing. Jenny gasped as she saw the FBI agents, with guns drawn, beginning to chase Chipper into the room. Then she heard Angus bark. She almost started laughing, then fear overwhelmed her. Condoleezza Rice's security guards were on the move, as well, toward Chipper but not with guns showing.

A few people started exiting the room, but most just stood or sat and watched what was happening. Chipper kept yelling, "Chemicals, Arabs, get out! Get out now!"

Stevens recognized Chipper and headed for the stage to get the microphone. Chipper was in the middle of the room still screaming, with the crowd not reacting, when Stevens grabbed the microphone and said, "Stay in your seats. This man is crazy. Security! Security! Grab that man. He's a lunatic!"

Angus found Jenny first and jumped up on her lap. Those at her table were amused. Stein looked at her and whispered, "I think we should leave the room. He wouldn't be doing this for no reason." Jenny, Stein, Debbie, and Kira started walking toward Chipper just as agent Lopez tackled Chipper and brought him to the floor. Jenny yelled, "Don't hurt him!" and screamed loudly again, "Don't hurt him!" Lopez had his knee on Chipper's neck and his arm pinned behind his back. Chipper was immobile.

Stevens said, "Take him outside and shoot him for all I care," into his microphone. Stein turned toward the stage and climbed the steps.

Stein replied, "Donald. Let's listen to what he has to say." Big Bill advanced toward where Lopez had Chipper on the floor and leaned over him and said, "Let him go. He's no threat. Let's hear what he has to say."

Chipper gasped at Bill, "Irene showed up, Bill. She's OK. She told me what's up." Big Bill grabbed Lopez by the shoulders and lifted him off of Chipper's neck. The other two agents had guns pointed at Bill. Bill knew they wouldn't fire in a crowded ballroom with so many people around. Jenny was now crying, and Kira was hugging her and holding her hand. Angus was now on top of the table and was sniffing the air, with his head pointed toward the ceiling. Angus started barking loudly and was disturbing all the plates and wine bottles. He was jumping up toward the ceiling while in the middle of the table. Jenny was yelling, "Angus! Angus!"

Lopez released his hold on Chipper and let him stand up. Big Bill, holding one of Chipper's arms, and Lopez, holding the other, led Chipper to the stage. Now, virtually everyone in the room was standing and paying rapt attention. The three FBI agents and Rice's two security guards were standing in front of the stage waiting eagerly for an explanation.

Stevens was reluctant to hand Chipper the microphone. Stein grabbed it out of his hand and handed it to Chipper. Stevens didn't look happy. He stepped to the side and waited, like everyone else in the room. Chipper started and spoke very quickly. He didn't say who he was but said, "I'm not sure how much time we have or how dangerous it is in this room. Everyone should get out. Ten days ago, my friend Irene McVay was kidnapped by the Arabs who bought the estate on the fourteenth fairway. She escaped. I don't know how yet, but she showed up on my back steps earlier this evening. I took her to Community Hospital. She was in a bad way. All she could say was 'Chemicals' and 'Clambake.' I think the Arabs are trying to kill everyone in this room and you should get out now." Then he screamed "Now!"

Many in the room started exiting in haste. Patrick Cantlay started running and tripped over a chair and fell to the ground. He screamed in pain. He got up but was holding his left wrist. All the other players gave him a bad time about trying to rush past them to get out of the room.

Stevens grabbed the microphone again and said, "Don't listen to this idiot. Just don't listen to him." Angus was now jumping up and down on the table and doing his best to act like a pointer, head toward the ceiling. Many were noticing it was getting warmer in the room than they expected and started taking off their jackets and sweaters.

Special agent Tripp whispered to agent Chan, who was a specialist in counterterrorism. Chan walked over to Jenny's table, grabbed a chair, and slowly made sure the table would hold his weight. Angus stopped barking. He stood on the table, and the room was silent. The first thing he said loudly was, "Does anyone else smell chicken coming from the heating vents near you?" Many wondered why this was appropriate but turned their heads towards the vents and smelled.

Stevens yelled, "We are NOT having chicken! No chicken!"

Many others started yelling. "I smell chicken!"

Chan took out of his coat pocket a MX908 handheld continuous area vapor chemical monitor. Before he held it at arm's length above him, he said, "We should NOT be smelling chicken. It is a commonly-used masking smell to cover up other chemicals." When he held up his device it started pinging off and on. Chan yelled, "Everyone out of this room immediately! Walk quietly, but get out as quickly as you can."

Agent Tripp now had the microphone and announced, "Special Agent Tripp, FBI. For your safety, get out of this room and get off this floor of the Inn. Whoever is in charge here, when everyone gets out, don't allow anyone on this floor until we give the all-clear. In the meantime, make sure the overhead sprinklers are activated and kept on for at least four hours. This Clambake is over!" Stevens groaned.

There was a rush to the doorways and down the stairs. Condoleezza's guards grabbed her and pushed through the crowd. Lopez let Chipper go, and Chipper quickly found Jenny. Jenny, again, was crying. She hugged him as hard as she could. They headed to the exits. They didn't worry about Angus. He would follow them and find his way out. He was a hero again.

The Grand Ballroom at the Inn at Spanish Bay was flooded soon after, similar to the ballroom at the Lodge at Pebble Beach.

HOSPITAL VISIT

Many in the crowd started ordering drinks at the bar in the lobby of the Inn. Chipper, Jenny, Richard Stein, Debbie Rogers, and Bill O'Shea managed to find each other in the lobby. Former Miss America Kira K. Dixon, was a few feet away, talking to admiring touring professionals. Bill was anxious to get over to the hospital to see how Irene was. No one was able to retrieve their cell phones. There was a lot of grumbling. Maybe tomorrow.

Chipper, Jenny, and Bill left their cars at the Inn and called Limo Driver Jim Tiffany, to pick them up at the Inn and take them to Community Hospital. He wasn't really available, it was a busy week, but he cancelled his other appointments and was soon in the parking circle outside the Inn at Spanish Bay. Stein and Debbie were anxious to go over to their new estate and see if the renting Arabs were still there. Debbie was reluctant and said, "They could be dangerous. I don't want to go, Richard." Stein insisted.

Chipper didn't feel like talking in the limo but was peppered continuously by Bill and Jenny. "How did Irene look? How did she escape? Did she say anything, other than about chemicals and the Clambake?" Chipper told them what he knew, which wasn't very much. There wasn't any small talk. Jenny clung to Chipper's arm. Angus curled up on Jenny's lap.

Jim left them off at the entrance to the emergency room and said he would wait and take Angus for a walk. Jenny and Chipper held hands as they walked in and were amused at how fast Bill was moving in front of them. They had never seen him move at any pace faster than a slow walk. He was jogging into the building. They could hear him ahead of them in the emergency room waiting area say, "Looking for Irene McVay. Where can I find Irene McVay?"

The receptionist beckoned him over and said, "And who are you?"

He seemed embarrassed when he said softly, "I'm her boyfriend."

The receptionist giggled when she said, "She can only have one visitor at a time, and she's with a few people now. We had to let them question her."

Chipper was at Bill's side when both at the same time said, "Who is she with?"

"There are a few policemen talking to her now, actually. And there is another man waiting to see her after them. I'm not sure the doctor will let you see her after all she's been through. Talking to the police might take a lot out of her. They just got here."

Chipper said, "Who else is waiting to see her?" Then he looked over in the corner of the waiting room and saw Jerry Devine from the Monterey Herald beginning to rise from his chair and come over to Chipper.

"I have nothing to say to you, Jerry. Really nothing. Why don't you let Irene rest? You can get your story tomorrow." Devine had his phone recording already and was snapping photos of Chipper.

"The news can't wait, Chipper. You know that. If you don't give me a story, I'll just make it up. I've already heard about the rumpus you caused at the Clambake."

"How did you know Irene was here, Devine?"

"I have my sources."

"Well, if you get in there, give her some rest. Let her alone. I have nothing to say to you." Devine was busy snapping pictures of Jenny now.

Chipper said to Jenny and Bill, "Let's go get something to eat at the snack bar and then come back later." Devine started to follow them out, but Big Bill stood in front of him and blocked his way. Devine took the hint and stayed in the waiting room.

The Community Hospital snack bar was renowned for having great food. Better than any hospital food anywhere. The Fountain Court Café was open until eight thirty, and seating was available around the beautiful inside fountain and pond. Many people went here rather than local restaurants. They each ordered the famous egg salad sandwich on wheat. Jenny and Chipper shared a chocolate milkshake, and Bill had one for himself. They ate quickly. Almost uncomfortably quickly. Big Bill let out a belch which was heard by most people in the vicinity.

As they were nearing the end of the meal, Chipper spotted Sheriff's Deputies Henderson and Anderson heading to the counter. He ran over to them and asked, "I assume you were the guys talking to Irene?"

Anderson was not eager to talk and just said, "We can't talk now, Blair. Just grabbing a quick coffee. It's going to be a long night. It's already been a long day. We have to go."

Chipper said, "Is Irene OK? Where are you headed?"

Anderson was silent but Henderson said, "She is surprisingly good for all she's been through. We're actually headed to the Hastings estate to check out her story. Going to be interesting over there. Can't tell you why, though."

Chipper just said, "Thanks. The Hastings estate is now Richard Stein's you know. Is Devine in with Irene now?"

Anderson said, "Yes. The fucker went in there right after us. He's in there for a long time, probably."

STEIN'S ESTATE

Richard Stein waited for his car at the valet outside the Inn at Spanish Bay. He was about tenth in line. It took a long time. Debbie wanted to walk home to their condo across the fairway, but Stein insisted she come along. Stein kept going up to the two valets, showing them his business card, and prodding them to get Stein's car first. "I'm the General Counsel of this goddamned Corporation. What is your name, son?" The valet ignored him. Shane Lowry said, "Pipe down, little guy. We're all important here."

When Stein finally got his bright yellow Lexus, it drew some whistles from the remaining crowd. Debbie got in the passenger side. Stein walked slowly to the driver's side, wearing his cowboy hat, and yelled at Lowry, "So long, sucker!" Lowry just laughed.

Debbie's first comment was, "Aren't you afraid, Richard, that your house is trashed or that the Arab renters might still be there? I'm more worried they will still be there. They villainously tried to kill everyone in the room. They certainly won't care about killing us."

Stein said, "You read too many mystery books, Debbie. We'll be fine." She was quiet the rest of the way to the estate. When they arrived, the gate was wide open, and Stein didn't hesitate to drive up to the front door. He honked the horn a few times so that, if someone was in the house, they would not be surprised. When he parked in front of the house, he saw the front door was wide open.

Debbie said, "You go in first, Richard. It might be booby-trapped. I'm going to wait right here in the car. You wave to me if all seems OK."

Stein said, "You don't care about me getting ambushed, then. Thanks a lot, Debbie." He walked very slowly to the front door and peeked in. He pushed the door completely open and then waited until he entered. He yelled, "Anyone here? Anyone here?" He cupped his ears with both hands and waited. There was no sound. He waved to Debbie it was OK to enter the house.

She was still reluctant, opened the car window, and said, "Go look at the rest of the house. I'm not going in there until you check more rooms."

Stein yelled, "You know how many rooms our estate has now, don't you? Might take a few days to check all the rooms! We have really arrived!" He walked around the first floor rooms, and the house looked unlived-in. There was no trace of anyone ever having used the house for the last several weeks. He was amazed. Stein went back to the front door and again waved Debbie in. This time she walked in.

Stein said, "I'll go check the upstairs. Why don't you go down to the wine cellar and get us a great bottle of champagne. Have you seen the amount of wine and champagne there is down there? It's a gold mine. We'll never be able to drink all that. Get the one that looks most expensive. It seems the house is finally ours. We can move in as quickly as we can." Stein then headed upstairs, and Debbie went down to the wine cellar.

As soon as Stein went in the master bedroom upstairs, he heard the most bloodcurdling scream from Debbie. He panicked and ran downstairs as fast as he could, assuming the worst: that someone was downstairs and had attacked her. As he reached the first floor, Debbie was running up the stairs and grabbed Richard. She was still screaming and could not stop. She was muttering, "It's awful. It's awful. I'm never coming in this house again." She continued screaming as she ran outside and stood next to the yellow Lexus.

Stein slowly tiptoed downstairs and peeked in the wine cellar. He was lucky he had been warned to expect the worst. He didn't scream but was taken aback by the two bodies and the immense amount of blood on the ground. He didn't have his cell phone yet, as it was still in some sort of storage at Spanish Bay. He ran back upstairs and used the landline phone. There was only one in the house, because it was needed to control the front gate. He called 911 and said, "Please get officers over to this address."

The 911 operator, after a few agonizing minutes wait, told him that there were deputy sheriffs already on the way to his house. He should expect them very soon. Stein hoped it would be Henderson and Anderson.

FBI AGENTS

Special Agent Tripp and his two sidekicks, Chan, and Lopez, ran to their car parked in the traffic circle at the Inn at Spanish Bay. They were relieved that Stevens had followed their instructions and that the Grand Ballroom was being flooded. Chan had used his MX908 handheld counter to comb the large first-floor area and declared it clean of chemical issues. They were headed to the Whitebread estate off the fourteenth fairway and called for backup. Tripp was expecting the worst and made sure SWAT teams from both Monterey and Seaside police departments were headed to the estate. He also contacted local FBI offices in Salinas and San Jose to start his way, as well. He didn't care if it was overkill. He knew he needed backup.

Tripp waited in his car, a block away from the Whitebread estate. They waited for only about ten minutes when Monterey SWAT arrived with two armored vehicles. The armored vehicles entered the open front gate first, with Tripp's car behind, and proceeded slowly up the driveway to the front door. Tripp saw two Dobermans and one Pit bull just sitting on the front steps. He was surprised the front door was open. The SWAT group and the FBI agents remained in their cars, while the dogs started barking wildly and pacing back and forth. They remained in their cars, immobilized by the dogs.

Tripp finally said to Lopez, "Get out of the car and do something about those dogs, Lopez."

Lopez laughed, "You get out and do something, Tripp. I'm not going out there." Tripp wasn't happy at all. While they stared at each other in silence, one of the SWAT team members in full tactical gear, wearing arm protectors on both arms, exited from the armored vehicle, and the dogs ran straight at him. He sprayed some sort of mace on the first Doberman, but the second grabbed his leg and started shaking back and forth. The man couldn't keep his balance and covered his face with both arms as he crumbled to the ground with the dogs attacking. Two other men immediately jumped out of the vehicle and started kicking the dogs violently and spraying more chemicals at them.

All three dogs headed toward the open front gate. Tripp called the SPCA and county animal control to make them aware of the situation. Seaside SWAT arrived, and now there were four armored vehicles in the driveway. Tripp and the others all exited and stood near the front door. Tripp's orders were for almost all to wait in place while Chan entered the house with two of the Monterey SWAT team. No one would enter until Chan had scanned the entire house for chemicals. The two SWAT team members were armed and would lead Chan through the house. Monterey SWAT handed Chan a bulletproof vest for additional protection.

Tripp and the outside group sat on the front steps and waited for over an hour until the inside group came back. Chan immediately said, "The house looks like no one has ever lived in it: no food, no towels, no sheets or anything on the beds. Completely empty, except for some furniture. No trace of anyone."

Tripp impatiently asked, "Any sign of chemicals?"

Chan nodded his head and said, "In one of the bedrooms in the guest wing downstairs, my device indicated chemical residue. That room was definitely used for something nepharious. The room has to be marked off and thoroughly cleaned. No one can spend more than ten minutes in that room without proper protective clothing and a gas mask."

Tripp asked, "Chan. Can we safely say, without a doubt, that the Arabs in this house were responsible for the attempted chemical attack on the Clambake tonight?"

"Yes, sir. We can say that," Chan replied.

"Where the hell are they now, then?" Tripp commented. "It's probably too late to ground the planes and blockade all the highways."

The Monterey SWAT coordinator picked up his phone and called, on his own hunch, the Monterey Airport private plane terminal. He was quickly put through to the manager and was told that a private plane, with an itinerary showing it was flying to Casablanca, was registered to a Tommy Whitebread. It was scheduled to depart at six thirty that evening. There were four Cadillac Escalades sitting near the runway in front of the terminal. The coordinator proudly walked up to Tripp and shared the information.

Tripp was quickly on his phone to FBI headquarters in Washington D.C. It was after midnight, but he was immediately put in touch with the sleeping Deputy Director, Paul Abbate, on a special phone. Abbate listened carefully as Tripp explained what had happened. Chan and Lopez waited patiently for the half-hour conversation. When Tripp was off the phone, his only comment was, "We're going to handle this. No problem."

DOCTOR HANSEN

After their quick meal, Chipper and Jenny returned to the emergency room, found Dr. Hansen, and peppered him with questions about Irene McVay. Bill was now in the room with Irene. Jenny and Chipper didn't want to bother them. If Hansen was able to answer their questions, they could just call Jim and head home. They would leave Bill at the hospital.

They went in the emergency room waiting area and asked for Dr. Hansen. He came out about ten minutes later. Jenny immediately said, "How is Irene?"

Hansen politely said, "It's lucky you brought her in when you did. She was severely dehydrated and malnourished. We gave her IV fluids and pain medication. She must be one tough lady. She has four cracked ribs. Very painful. There is nothing we can do about those. They will heal in time. We'll monitor her pain medication and keep her in the ICU for observation for probably a week. She has other assorted bruises and contusions on many parts of her body, particularly her sides and shoulders. She has been through hell. Did I already say what a tough cookie she is? The most concern is her concussion. We did a CT scan to see if she had any swelling or bleeding. Luckily, there does not seem to be. We have to do a series of cognitive and memory tests to see how bad the concussion is. She may be dizzy and disoriented for quite a while. She can't live by herself. I suggest a live-in nurse for at least a month. It's best to be safe on these kind of things."

"That won't be a problem," Jenny said. "I can arrange that. I'll visit her often."

Chipper asked, "Did she tell you her story? She was kidnapped by the Arabs, right? How did she escape?"

Hansen said, "We didn't want to traumatize her more than she already is. We left that to the police. We're not going to ask her any questions about that. We just want her to rest and heal as quickly as possible."

Chipper was quiet, but Jenny asked, "What can we do for her now?"

"Not much, really. When she gets home, she'll need support."

Chipper asked, "Are you going to have a psychologist or psychiatrist come and talk to her? You have them on staff that are good?"

"Yes, we'll wait a few days, then do that. In the plan."

Chipper and Jenny called Jim, then headed outside to meet him. Angus was in the back seat of the limo and again just climbed on Jenny's lap and tried to fall asleep.

ANDERSON AND HENDERSON

Debbie Rogers was cowering in the driveway when Anderson and Henderson's police car came up the driveway. When they exited the car, she ran over to them and just said, "Thank God. Thank God you are here."

Anderson said, "We understand there are some bodies in the wine cellar?"

She again said, "Thank God you are here." She was shaking. Anderson didn't care and rushed past her into the house. Henderson stayed back and asked if he could do anything for her. She again said, "Just so I don't ever have to go in that house again. I'll never go in that house again." Henderson then jogged past her to catch up with his partner. Stein met them in the foyer.

Henderson said, "Hi, Richard. Nice to see you again. It seems there are some dead bodies in your new house wine cellar? We spoke to Irene McVay at the hospital. She is in a bad way but was lucid and told us the whole story. Strong woman. She bravely did a number on these guys! Hard to believe that. How old is she?"

Stein said, "I think she is 59," as they headed down the steps to the wine cellar. When they got to the bottom of the steps and saw the carnage, Stein repeated Henderson's comment, "She did, in fact, do a number on these guys. I wonder how she did that. Really amazing."

Henderson told Stein to stay near the entrance while they wandered inside and took a closer look. Henderson said, "We are expecting the coroner. We'll have to be here awhile to sort things out. You and your friend outside should probably just go home now. We'll do the rest."

Stein asked, "When might I be able to hire someone to clean this mess up? I hope the blood comes up off the ground. I might have to just put a new floor over this mess."

Anderson said, "Stein, you'll have to leave this room as is until there is a trial. Might be six months."

"You are kidding me. Why would there even be a trial? You're not going to accuse Irene McVay of murder? She was just trying to get out, justifiably, to get away from her kidnappers. Self-defense. Certainly improbable but understandable that she did this. She is a hero. If she didn't escape, the entire Clambake crowd may have perished."

Anderson said, "I certainly don't want to mess with her. Especially if she has a bottle of wine in her hand. These guys are a mess. Look at that chainsaw. Watch out for all that glass. We have to dust for prints, and hopefully this dead guy here has the only prints on it."

Henderson added, "You know, your girlfriend never wants to come in this house again. You are going to have a hard time getting her in this room. Probably have a hard time getting her to set foot on the property ever!"

Anderson commented, "Go home, Mr. Stein. Just go to your other home. We'll contact you when you can come back in this house. What are you going to do with this huge estate, anyway? It's too big for anyone."

Stein walked away, grabbed Debbie in the driveway and tried to console her, then headed to their condo.

Anderson and Henderson waited for the coroner and wandered the entire property, trying to find the escape route that Irene had mumbled to them. They found some blood, Irene's, on the way to the back gate. There was no question her story was valid.

MONTEREY HERALD

Special Agent Tripp smiled broadly when he read the morning Monterey Herald newspaper headline. Jerry Devine was upset that his article on Irene's escape was relegated to the bottom of the second page and his story about the Clambake debacle was in smaller print several pages back. He considered it the story of the year and didn't know why it wasn't given the main headlines. Tripp picked up the paper and saw a banner headline with an AP byline.

MONTEREY PLANE DOWN NEAR FLORIDA
-----ASSOCIATED PRESS

A private chartered airplane that took off from the Monterey Airport last night at about 6:30, was reported missing, and presumed down, in the Southern Atlantic Ocean, about 300 miles off the East Coast of Florida. The last recorded sound from the aircraft was the MAYDAY signal from either the pilot or copilot, with no explanation about the MAYDAY distress call.

The plane manifest indicated that the plane was chartered by a Mr. Whitebread, no first name given, and had 16 passengers. It was headed to Casablanca, Morocco.

It was the first plane departing Monterey Airport that has crashed since July 13, 2021, when a twin-engine Golden Eagle Cessna, piloted by

74-year-old Mary Carlin of Pacific Grove, crashed into a home just south of the Monterey Airport. It was reported at the time that she became disoriented. She died in the crash.

Surveillance planes sent to the scene of last night's crash were able to see a debris field covering a large area. The extent of the airplane damage indicates that there are certainly no survivors of this horrific crash.

There is currently no listed cause of the plane crashing, but the FAA is investigating.

Tripp didn't read any further. He knew the reason the plane went down and was proud to be an FBI agent and proud of his channels of communication with FBI headquarters in Washington D.C. He felt justice was served: swiftly and correctly. He turned the page and saw Devine's articles on both Irene's escape and the Clambake debacle.

MONTEREY HERALD

MISSING PEBBLE BEACH WOMAN FOUND
BYLINE JERRY DEVINE

Irene McVay, the Pebble Beach socialite, who had been missing for ten days, showed up, unexpectedly, last evening, on the back steps of Chipper Blair's estate, off the fourteenth fairway of Pebble Beach Golf Course. It seems Mr. Blair is at the center of every controversy and mystery that happens in the Del Monte Forest. Mr. Blair refused to comment, but the accompanying photograph shows a surprised and obviously upset Mr. Blair and his wife, Jenny Nelson, in the waiting room of the hospital.

I was able to do the only exclusive interview of Ms. McVay while she was lapsing in and out of consciousness in the emergency room at the Community Hospital of the Monterey Peninsula. She was incoherent much of the time, but she was able to impart some factual information about her captivity.

She remembers visiting the estate next to Blair's home and walking in the front door unannounced. Then she remembers being held behind a locked door in some sort of food pantry. She survived on pita bread but doesn't know for how many days. At some point she was beaten and kicked. She never saw any of her captors.

At some point she was shoved in a car, beaten more, and taken to another estate. She was blindfolded and in pain. She woke up in a familiar room: the wine cellar of her society friend Emily Hastings. Ms. Hastings no longer owned the home, and the current owner is Pebble Beach Company General Counsel,

Richard Stein. Stein says he rented the house for three weeks to a group visiting for the ATT golf tournament.

Although highly unlikely due to her small size, she claims she was able to hit her captors with bottles of champagne and managed to escape out the back gate of the former Hastings estate. She remembers meeting some golfers on one of the holes at Pebble Beach and being driven down some fairways until she recognized a familiar estate. She then exited the golf cart and ended up, of course, on the back steps of Chipper Blair's house.

The emergency room physician, Dr. Hansen, detailed her injuries as extensive: severe dehydration, malnutrition, four broken ribs, a concussion, and other assorted bruises and contusions.

Whether her story is fabricated or truthful may never be known.

BEHIND THE SCENES

At the Inn at Spanish Bay after the crowd had cleared out, Pebble Beach CEO Donald Stevens, ATT Tournament Director Steve John, and PGA Tour Commissioner Jay Monahan had adjourned to the Sticks restaurant space and were sipping on expensive Scotch. The restaurant was empty, and Stevens had gone behind the bar to find the Scotch and some glasses: no ice, no water, just Scotch. Richard Stein followed them in, out of curiosity, and said, "I'd like to sit in if you need any legal advice." They allowed him to stay, which would end up being beneficial to Richard.

Monahan started and spoke in a whisper, even though they were the only ones in the room, "It is important that this conversation goes no further than the four of us. In fact, this conversation never happened." The other three nodded approval and Monahan continued, "We all think that the Arab group that was here, supposedly named Whitehead, were responsible for this, but there is really no proof. It is important that we downplay this. We don't want this incident to ruin our entire plan for the LIV and PGA merger."

Stevens interrupted, "What exactly are the plans for the merger?"

Monahan replied, "I can't tell you that, Donald, but this incident may get me some advantage in the negotiations. If word of this ever got out, the merger would never take place."

Stevens said loudly, "But Jay, these guys, these bad operators, just tried to kill you and the best players on the PGA tour. How can you even face these guys?"

"I'm not going to answer that question, Donald. We're already too far down the road. The PGA tour depends on their money now. It's a whole new ballgame. Now how do we keep this quiet?"

Steve John said, "I'll call the Herald. I know the editor. They don't have many writers left. I'm sure Jerry Devine is on the story. I'll have the editor tone down his story and move it back in the paper. I'll make sure there are no online articles. No one reads the Herald anymore, anyway. Just a few locals who don't have the energy to cancel. I'll call her when we are done here. I don't anticipate any problems. We bring in a lot of advertising when they do the tournament magazine."

Monahan said, "Thank you, Steve. I can handle the PGA tour members. They exited and don't really know who might have done this. I'll tell them to just ignore it. They will. How about your staff, Donald? Can you keep them quiet? Who was the wild man who came in and disrupted everything? Can you control him?"

Stein said, "Sir, that wild man saved everyone in there. If it wasn't for him, we might all be dead!"

Stevens said, "Stein, I told you that you could sit in, but I don't want you saying anything more. I'll handle Blair."

Stein saw an opportunity and said, "You know, chief, if you fire him, he'll go to the press and tell everything he knows. Why don't you just put him back on the Pebble range, where he wants to be, and I'll handle Chipper? He just wants to hit golf balls, he won't care about telling anyone about this. He's a good guy."

Stevens just said, "I'll think about it. Give me a day."

Stein was emboldened and asked, "What about the Whitebread estate, next door to Chipper's? I wonder what's going to happen to that. Maybe they'll sell it now."

Stevens said, "I don't really care, Stein. Just do your job. I don't think we need you in here anymore."

Stein left the meeting. He was in his office early the next morning. He had read the Monterey Herald article about the plane crash. His first phone call, before seven AM, was to Special Agent Tripp. "Hello Agent Tripp, this is Richard Stein, General Counsel of the Pebble Beach Corporation…"

Tripp interrupted and said, "I know who you are, Stein. Do you just enjoy saying your title all the time? Why are you calling so early? I'm still in bed. Haven't had my coffee yet. It was a very late night. I was up until two AM. We finished at the Whitebread estate, then went over to look at your place when Anderson called us. What a mess. This is a messy business. What do you want?"

"I read the article about the plane crash. Just wondering if you knew if that was our Arab friends from the Whitebread estate? Are they all dead?"

Tripp said, "I don't know anything about that Stein. I haven't even seen anything about that. What happened? Let me get the Herald, and then I'll call you back."

Stein waited thirty minutes, then he impatiently called Tripp. Tripp didn't pick up, so Stein called him three more times until Tripp finally answered, "Stein, I told you I would call you back."

"Did you read about the plane crash? Quite a coincidence, right?" Tripp didn't say a word, so Stein continued, "Quite a coincidence! Let me ask you a hypothetical question. Suppose all the Whitebreads are dead. I know the property they purchased for cash was bought by the Sovereign Wealth Fund of the Saudi's, but the property is under the name Todd Whitebread. This is a made-up name of a man who is almost certainly dead. So my question is: what is the status of the property?"

Tripp simply said, "You are the attorney, Stein. I don't really care now.

Good riddance to them. You do what you have to do. I'm out of this. I don't care."

Stein smiled to himself and then hung up. His next phone call was to his Superior Court Judge friend, who had done him so many favors before. He thought awhile before calling Cindy Springer. "Cindy. How would you like to live in, and possibly own, the Hastings estate?"

Stein expected a reaction but waited for several seconds before Cindy started yelling excitedly on the other end of the phone. She finally said, "And how would that be possible, Richard? Just how can that happen?"

Stein said, "Let's meet, and I'll explain everything to you, Cindy. I own the house now, and I bought it at a bargain price. I can give you a great deal on it. I think Debbie and I are going to move into the estate next door to Chipper's. With the NIL money that you have coming in, you can certainly afford it." Cindy started yelling again.

Stein's next call was to the Pebble Beach Corporation maintenance crew. He arranged for a team of employees to thoroughly clean both his own estate and the Whitebread estate. Things were falling into place.

JENNY AND CHIPPER

Chipper left early the next morning, on his three golf course route, to work at Spanish Bay. It was raining again, cold, and miserable. Jenny didn't know how he still played golf enthusiastically in this weather. She was reading the short Herald article, hidden in the back pages of the paper and wasn't happy.

MONTEREY HERALD

CLAMBAKE PARTY INTERRUPTUS
BYLINE JERRY DEVINE

This year's annual festive Clambake dinner, for participants of the ATT golf tournament, was rolling along with great entertainment from country stars Darius Rucker and Clay Walker when our friend Chipper Blair came running in with his little black dog and sent everyone home.

The banter between tournament chairman Steve John and non-playing celebrities Bill Murray and Ray Romano was lively and kept the all-star crowd laughing most of the evening. There was no explanation of why Blair came running in yelling, "Get out! Get out!" Although there was no explanation, everyone did get out, and the party ended early. Many participants saw men in black suits testing the air quality of the room.

Rumor has it that he was upset he was not invited, as his wife, teaching professional Jenny Nelson, was going to be presented an award for making the top-fifty list in Golf Digest magazine's annual teaching pro national rankings.

No one I attempted to interview for this story was willing to talk: from PGA professionals to Pebble Beach Corporation employees to PGA Tour staff. Chipper Blair declined an interview, as well. I will continue to investigate this breaking story.

Jenny decided to drive to Spanish Bay and show Chipper the article before she went to work at Spyglass Hill. Because of the rain and the tournament, she didn't have any lessons but was going in to see if she could help with anything. It might be a restful day.

She parked in front of the entrance path to the clubhouse, entered the front door, walked along the plush carpet, and went out the back door, overlooking the first tee at Spanish Bay golf course. She could see Chipper's protective tent, and the rain was coming down hard, but Chipper was on the first tee, taking some practice swings with his driver. She ran down the steps, keeping the Herald article under her windbreaker so it would remain dry. She ducked into the tent and watched Chipper hit three drives before he walked back under cover. He was soaked but gave her a big hug anyway. She pushed him away and laughed.

Jenny said, "You have to look at the Devine Herald article." She took the article and watched as Chipper read it. Then she said, "You aren't upset?"

"Not really," he said, "What did you expect? Someone got to Devine and the paper, obviously."

Jenny shook her head from side to side, "My Chipper. Of course you aren't upset. You and Angus saved the lives of everyone in the room: the entire group of elite players on the tour, some of the most important and famous entertainers in the U.S., the Pebble Beach Corporation managers and staff, and you don't even care about being recognized as a hero."

"The only one I wanted to save was you, Jenny. The others didn't matter. Kira, maybe. Conde Rice, maybe. I don't care about the recognition. I just want to be back on the range at Pebble. I'm hoping Stevens puts me back there next week. Whether he does or not, that's where I will be on Monday. I love you, Jenny Nelson."

"You are soaking wet, Chipper. You look like Angus in the rain. Get a towel and dry yourself."

"No reason to do that. With no one playing, I'll be out there again in a bit to hit more balls. I might even head down the fairway to pick them up."

"See you later, Mr. Chips," Jenny said, then took off running up the stairs and through the clubhouse to get to her car.

THE MONTEREY COUNTY WEEKLY

The next day, the first day of the golf tournament, when she read the Monterey County Weekly Squid column, Jenny was even more upset.

THE SQUID FRY

The Squid has been watching closely the interesting story about Pebble Beach socialite Irene McVay. She had been missing and unaccounted for almost ten days. The local authorities had been looking for her. The FBI had been called in. Speculation around Chipper Blair and Irene McVay's will filled the Del Monte Forest with rumors. If you can believe it, McVay turned up on Blair's back steps. What are the chances? Really, what are the chances?

The story, which I tend not to believe, was that she was kidnapped by Arabs. I am not making this up. Then she escaped. The Squid is skeptical. Skeptical Squid. Blair won't talk, while McVay is in the ICU recuperating. This story smells like dead fish. Squid can't wait to see what McVay spills when she is out of the ICU. What a fine kettle of fish you've gotten yourself into now, Blair.

When Jenny read the article, she immediately called the Monterey County Weekly to complain.

"I would like to talk to the Squid, please," she started.

The woman on the other end answered, "No one talks to the Squid. No one even knows who the Squid is. What do you want?"

"Whoever the Squid is, is printing lies and innuendo that is not true."

"So what else is new? The Squid writes a gossip column."

"But it has to be true, doesn't it?"

"It's all for fun, honey. It's all gossip."

"Well, this isn't fun at all, and don't call me honey. Let me talk to the publisher." Jenny was surprised when she was transferred immediately to Erik Cushman, the publisher of the Monterey County Weekly.

"What can I help you with?" he said, politely.

"Your Squid column is printing things that are not true!"

Cushman said, "So, what else is new?"

"Whoever the Squid is, cannot do that."

"Who am I speaking with?" Cushman continued.

"This is Jenny Nelson. I am Chipper Blair's wife. The Squid is implying he kidnapped poor Irene McVay. She is also a good friend."

Cushman said loudly, "Boy oh boy, you have your hands full with that one, don't you?"

Jenny said, "All he wants to do is play golf. He's a very nice man who tries to avoid trouble."

"He's not doing a very good job at that, obviously. I read the column before it was printed. The Squid just said they were skeptical. How could Irene McVay turn up on Chipper's back door steps?"

"Because she trusts him. The conspiracy theory that the Squid is speculating on is totally false. My husband is a hero. He saved everyone at the Clambake party. Everyone could have died. Talk to anyone that was there. Talk to the FBI."

Cushman then impolitely hung up on Jenny. She was livid.

THE ATT SIGNATURE EVENT

Jenny was angry that Chipper wasn't angry. She felt he was a hero, but he didn't care at all. He didn't care that he was getting bad publicity in both the Herald and the Weekly. Chipper was anxious each morning during the golf tournament to just drive to the very quiet confines of the first tee at Spanish Bay. He spent most of the day alone but not lonely. He was enjoying it. Most people were watching the golf at Pebble and Spyglass. Chipper had plenty of time to hit balls down the wide first fairway then go pick them up in his cart. There were a few groups teeing off each morning, and a few more in the afternoon.

Thursday, the rain stayed away. The pros played lift, clean, and place. Thomas Detry shot 63 at Spyglass, and sore-wristed Patrick Cantlay, or Can't Play, as Chipper called him, managed a 64 at Spyglass. Very surprising due to his sore wrist caused by trying to beat everyone out of the Grand Ballroom at Spanish Bay two evenings before. Best score at Pebble was a 65 by last week's tour winner, Mathew Pavon.

Friday, there were mild showers. Eight of the nine leaders were lucky to play Spyglass on Thursday and Pebble on Friday. It really wasn't fair. World number 1, Scottie Scheffler, shot 64. Newcomer Ludvig Aberg shot 65, both at Pebble Beach. Cantlay was lurking with a 70, and Justin Thomas was in contention with a 67. Chipper didn't care.

Saturday was a no-wind, wet day, the third day in a row of lift, clean, and place. Everyone played Pebble Beach. Wyndham Clark made every putt he looked at: 360 feet worth, a miracle putting day, and shot a course record, 60, by two strokes. Jason Day shot 63 on Pebble.

Sunday, the deluge arrived with heavy wind. Spectators were not allowed. Play was suspended for the day, and then the tournament was cancelled on Monday. Too dangerous; too much wind and too wet. Wyndham Clark, who was leading by only one over Ludvig Aberg, was declared the winner of the title, along with the 3.6 million dollar first prize. This time, Chipper cared.

THE PEBBLE BEACH DRIVING RANGE

When Chipper heard early that the tournament was cancelled, he looked out the back window of his estate, and heaved a sigh of relief. The lights from the back deck illuminated the back yard and the fourteenth fairway at Pebble Beach. He was anxious to get going back to his driving range. He didn't care if he wasn't officially assigned back there; that's where he was going. There was a slight drizzle, but it didn't matter. Jenny was still sleeping, and Angus was circling Chipper's bare feet excitedly. Angus could feel the excitement.

Chipper pointed to Jenny, still asleep on the bed, and Angus knew what he meant. Angus leaped on the bed and started licking Jenny's face to wake her up. Although groggy, she hugged Angus and looked at Chipper, who was walking toward the bed. "I guess you want me up now, right?"

"You got it, Jenny. I need to get going early. Lots of stuff to do at the range, I'm sure. It's probably a mess."

After dressing, all three headed out in the dark and mist. Angus was bounding along, comfortable that he didn't sense the evil dogs next door. His attitude was infectious. Although it was cold outside, both Jenny and Chipper were ready to hit their morning shots and get the day started. Jenny took a few practice swings with the brassie, hit a solid shot she knew would be about twenty feet to the right of the pin, exactly pin high, and did a little jig as Angus took off like a rocket toward the fourteenth green.

Chipper waited until Angus returned with the Slazenger and treated the energetic dog with seven treats. Chipper took a few swings with the spoon and eagerly followed the ball until it disappeared in the gloom. He also knew he had hit a good shot, probably about the same length away as Jenny's. Before Angus even came back, Chipper had hugged Jenny, and they agreed to meet at the Pebble driving range at noon. Jenny was hoping the weather was OK and she could complete her lesson with Cindy Springer. It had been a week since they had met for a noon lesson.

Chipper treated Angus again, then took off in his cart out to the fourteenth fairway. Jenny was surprised when Chipper appeared to be kneeling on the ground next to his cart and patting the fairway with his right hand. His mouth was moving, but she couldn't tell what he was saying. As she headed back to the house with Angus, she muttered out loud to the dog, "I certainly married a strange one, and I wouldn't have it any other way. And I love you, too, Angus."

If she could have heard Chipper, she wouldn't have been too surprised. As he was patting the turf he was saying, "Don't feel too bad, old girl. I can tell you feel embarrassed that someone shot 60 on you. It was lift, clean, and place. Just try to forget about it. You are still the greatest." Chipper could feel the course sighing, and she was embarrassed.

Chipper played fourteen and fifteen, his usual holes, then decided that he would just finish the last three also. He didn't care if anyone saw him on the course. Pebble Beach needed the love. On each hole, he got down on his knees and did the same speech, both on the tee and in the middle of the fairway. By the time he holed out for par on the eighteenth, he was sure he had made his friend, Pebble Beach Golf Course, feel better. She had certainly made him feel better. It was a glorious, wet, drizzly, damp, perfect morning.

The light was just coming up when Chipper arrived at the range. He spent three hours replacing divots, picking up tees, moving the tee blocks, picking up debris, and walking up and down the sides of the range chipping balls back into the middle so they could be picked up with the range wagon later in the day. He went into the shack and cleaned up the buckets, swept out the debris, and made sure the cash register was still working. His back was aching a bit. His last chore was making sure he put a bunch of broken tees and some dirt into the range machine to ensure it wouldn't work. The range needed a real attendant.

He finally was ready to swing the clubs to loosen up his back. No one had come to the range, but it seemed the rain was going way, and the sun was trying to finally come out. He was hoping Jenny and Cindy would show up. He started hitting some wedges toward the 100-yard marker but after exactly ten shots he heard Cindy Springer's voice from behind him. He turned, and she was running up, carrying her clubs on her back. Duncan was right behind her.

"Chipper! Chipper! Chipper! It's so good to see you. So good! I have so much to tell you. It's so exciting. So exciting. Chipper! Chipper! Chipper!"

Chipper was smiling but was shaking his head from side to side. He tried to say something, but Cindy continued, "Duncan and I are getting the Hastings estate. Well, really, half of it. But we are going to be the owners. We're going to be living in Pebble Beach and own an estate. It's beautiful! Just beautiful! Remember when we had a fancy dinner there? It has a long driveway and a statue in the middle, near the front door. It has tons of rooms. Just tons. A wine cellar. Can you believe it? Can you really believe it?"

Duncan was quiet and laughing behind Cindy. Chipper finally said, "How did this happen?"

"Richard is handling it all. He is so good to us. He says I have enough

NIL money coming in that we can afford half the house. He is doing all the paperwork, and he'll just take the payments out of the NIL money when it comes in. He said Debbie doesn't want to live in the house for some reason. Richard is buying the house next door to you. He and Debbie will be your neighbors. Isn't that great? He said something about the previous owner being dead and not really being the legal owner in the right name. I didn't understand half of what he was telling me. All he kept saying was he was getting a great deal. Great deal!"

Chipper put his finger over Cindy's mouth to quiet her and finally said, "Cindy, you should have another lawyer check all the paperwork."

She moved his finger to the side and said, "Too late, Chipper. Duncan and I have signed everything. I trust Richard. We own an estate in Pebble Beach. Who would have thunk it? Richard is having it cleaned now, and we can move in soon. Very soon. I'm so excited! I'm so excited! And you'll be right next door to Richard and Debbie."

All Chipper could say was, "Swell." Then he went back to hitting balls. Cindy started warming up next to him, and Duncan was behind filming her. She was all in Nike clothes this time. When Chipper looked behind her, he saw the usual gathering for about thirty college guys congregating at the back of the range. They were all sitting politely, with no yelling or screaming or beer that he could see. That changed, however, when Jenny came driving up and got out of her Jaguar. Chipper couldn't help feeling pride as the college guys started yelling at Jenny and Cindy now.

He thought to himself, *"Everything appears to be back to normal, finally."*

Jenny came up to Chipper and gave him a big hug and a kiss on the lips. She stood on her toes and raised her right leg a little behind her. The college guys all groaned. She turned around and gave them all a wink. Then she got serious about Cindy's lesson. Chipper hit balls next to Cindy and was impressed with how solidly she was hitting it.

Near the middle of the lesson, Big Bill O'Shea came striding up. He filled them all in on Irene's condition. She was moving out of ICU tomorrow. She was still a little fuzzy-brained but was out of danger physically. She was happy she was down to her high school weight and was looking forward to being finally at home. Big Bill knew she was getting back to normal when she asked if Mr. Takahashi could bring her some of his products to test. Jenny said, "Too much information, Bill."

Bill grabbed a few of Chipper's clubs and started hitting balls next to Chipper. Bill asked Chipper, "Aren't you upset at all the negative comments you are getting in the newspapers? We all know you are the hero in all of this."

"That's all that matters, Bill."

OLD BEN MORRIS

Chipper felt blessed and comfortable. He was surrounded by his love and his friends on the driving range. The sun was beaming through the clouds, and as he hit a very solid driver, Chipper Blair followed it with his eyes and thought of Old Ben Morris.

"First ya' picture it in the sky, laddie, against the cypress and the pine and the clouds. Then ya' hit the ball exactly where ya' see it, and it flies where the maker in heaven can count the dimples. And he's smilin' as much as you are at the freedom...at the beauty. Nothin' can compare, laddie."

*If you enjoyed this story about Chipper Blair and Jenny Nelson,
and their continuing golf-related adventures in the Del Monte Forest,
near Pebble Beach Golf Course, then be ready for the fifth book in
the series, Hopeful at the Hay, which will be published soon.*

Printed in the United States
by Baker & Taylor Publisher Services